BLOODLETTING
A Tale of Revenge

by
Andy Rausch

Burning Bulb
PUBLISHING

Bloodletting: A Tale of Revenge
By **Andy Rausch**

Burning Bulb Publishing
P.O. Box 4721
Bridgeport, WV 26330-4721
United States of America
www.BurningBulbPublishing.com

Cover designed by Gary Lee Vincent with the following licensed elements from Fotolia:
   - B – Lettre – violence, massacre, tuerie © DURIS Guillaume

First Burning Bulb Publishing printing.

Paperback Edition ISBN: 978-0-69223-146-3
Printed in the United States of America

DAY ONE

Joe Gibson arrived home from his trip, exhausted. It had been a long fucking day. As he made his way through the house, he had no sense that anything was out of the ordinary. When his wife didn't answer, he thought nothing of it. Maybe she hadn't heard him.

When Joe walked into the kitchen, he had no choice but to see things the way they were. He saw the three men standing around her, pistols in their hands. He looked to Denise, tied up and gagged, sitting in the kitchen on a wooden dining room chair. Her hair still wet from her shower, she wore a silk robe, closed so Joe couldn't see if she had anything on underneath.

Caught off guard, he could do nothing to help his wife before being struck in the back of the head with the pistol of the fourth man—the one he hadn't seen. Joe fell to the floor, hitting his head on the kitchen cabinet as he went down. On the floor, confused, disoriented, in shock and in pain, no idea what the fuck was happening. He had blood in his eyes. He tried to raise himself, wiping away the blood with his arm.

The fourth man was on him again, kicking him in the side. More pain, and Joe found himself on the ground again. He looked up at the men through blurry eyes. "What the fuck?" he said, the men laughing at him.

Now Joe got a good look at the men for the first time, but recognized no one. They were dressed identically, each wearing an expensive-looking suit with no tie, a dress shirt beneath opened at the top. They each wore black leather gloves. The clothes looked out of place on these men, each of whom looked rough and rugged like cons. One of the men was a big muscular

1

Mexican (about fifty years old) with a hideous v-shaped scar reaching down from above his left eyebrow through an apparently dead eye (complete with a tattooed teardrop) to his cheek and back up past the eyebrow to his forehead. Joe knew nothing concrete about this menacing man and yet he had the sense he was a stone cold killer.

The second man, a forty-something white guy with a pockmarked cop face and slicked-back black hair, was stocky with a build equal parts muscle and fat, he looked like a mean sonofabitch.

The third man was dark black with wild Don King hair and big, crazy wide eyes. Wiry, younger than the others, something about him suggested he'd just been released from prison.

The fourth man—the dirty bastard who'd struck Joe from behind and kicked him in the side—was a tall, gangly white guy with a high forehead, bug eyes, long hair, and a skinny head. He looked like Ichabod Crane from that old *Sleepy Hollow* cartoon. Joe figured him for about forty-five, and found him to be extremely creepy.

Looking at Denise, her beautiful eyes now big and afraid, filled with tears, staring at him, Joe felt re-energized. He scrambled to his knees in the hopes of rushing the men, but Ichabod kicked him back to the floor. Joe whirled around quickly to find himself face to face with the barrel of the man's pistol. His eyes moved upward to Ichabod's face. He could see clearly this man wanted to shoot him. "Do it," the man said, practically begging. "Go ahead and try that shit."

"Now, now," said Pockmarked Cop Face. "No need for that. I'm sure Mr. Gibson will do exactly as he's asked. Isn't that right, Joe?"

Joe looked at Denise sitting there helplessly, gagged and tied, her eyes pleading for him to save them both. He looked at Ichabod, his pistol still aimed at his face. Fuck. He felt like a pussy, but he could do nothing. Attacking the men now would be foolish and would only endanger Joe and his wife. No, he thought, he would wait until the right opportunity presented itself. Then, when he could get the drop on one of them, he would just have to hope for the best.

"All you gotta do is keep your fucking mouth shut and listen to what I have to say, Joe," Pockmarked Cop Face said, clearly enjoying the sound of his own voice. "Now I don't want to be unfriendly—especially when I'm a guest in someone else's home. It's just that we have a lot of ground to cover. So if I come across as anything less than cordial, I hope you'll forgive me. First we gotta get one thing straight—you make any wrong moves or try any Bruce Willis hero shit, things are gonna get real ugly real quick."

Pockmarked Cop Face caressed Denise's cheek with his pistol. "I'd hate to have to kill your wife, Joe."

The two men's eyes locked for a moment, Joe glaring so intently the man's smile fell away. "You hurt her," Joe said, "and I'll kill you. Maybe not today, maybe not tomorrow, but you will die."

This caused the other three gunmen to laugh hysterically. Pockmarked Cop Face didn't find it funny. "Big words coming from a guy who's on his knees with a gun to his head, don't ya think? We could all take turns raping your wife and I don't think there's a damned thing you could do about it, Joe." This caused the men to laugh harder.

The big Mexican spoke up. "I just got out of the joint, man. I could go for that." Pockmarked Cop Face looked to the Don King-looking motherfucker, who grabbed his crotch and said, "Sure, I'd fuck her." This caused the men to burst into laughter again. Finally Pockmarked Cop Face raised his hand, signaling them to stop.

3

He looked at Joe. "Let's skip the bullshit, Joe. No one's gonna rape your old lady. That's not why we're here. You keep cool and everything's gonna be just fine."

"Who are you?"

"Who I am is the asshole who's got you by the balls, friend. And I'm here to offer you an opportunity."

Joe's eyes narrowed. *"Opportunity?"*

"Yes. The opportunity for you to do something for us."

"Why would I want to do anything for you?"

"Good question. You what know what interests me? Motives. The reasons people do the things they do. I'm big on motives, Joe, and right now you need one. Why would you do anything for us? I'll give you two reasons."

"Okay?"

"The first is right here." Pockmarked Cop Face aimed his .45 at Denise's head. "And the second reason? The second reason got out of school at three o' clock."

And for the first time since all of this began, Joe remembered his daughter, Emily. The realization washed over him, and he felt guilty for not having noticed her absence sooner. But he'd been startled, and a lot had happened in the passing of the last five minutes. Joe felt his eyes filling up with tears. "Where is she?"

"Don't worry," said Pockmarked Cop Face. "She's safe."

"Please don't hurt her." Joe heard himself speak, surprised by the desperation in his voice.

"If you do what I ask you, there shouldn't be any problems. You ever play Simon Says, Joe? Sure you have. Okay, I'm Simon. That pretty much makes you my bitch. That means I tell you to do something—*anything*—you better damned well do it. Normally there's no prize in Simon Says, but we got us here a high stakes game, Joe. Go ahead, ask me what the prize is." He stared at Joe, but Joe said nothing. "Maybe you're thinking it's a new car. Is it a new car, Don Pardo?"

"No," Ichabod said, getting into the act. "It ain't a new car."

Joe stared at his wife, making eye contact with her, trying to tell her everything would be all right.

"Maybe an all-expense paid trip to the Bahamas?" said Pockmarked Cop Face.

"No," said the Don King-looking motherfucker. "It ain't that shit, neither."

"You know what the grand prize is, Joe? It's your eight-year-old daughter's life. If you don't do exactly what I tell you, little Emily goes down for the dirt nap."

"What do you want me to do?"

Pockmarked Cop Face smiled. "I'm gonna leave you with a folder. It'll be inside your car, underneath the driver's side floor mat. Inside that folder you will find a photograph of a man—a very bad man—and the address and room number of the hotel where he'll be staying, as well as a complete itinerary of his visit to New York."

Joe didn't understand. "What does he have to do with me?"

"Nothing. And everything."

"What does that mean?"

"It means that, as of now, he has absolutely nothing to do with you. But your futures are inextricably intertwined, Joe. You see, you're going to kill him."

Joe didn't understand what he was hearing. *"What?"*

"Murder him. Terminate with extreme prejudice. Take his life. Cash in his chips. Make him have one really bad fucking day."

"Why me? I'm no killer."

"Precisely the reason. Who's gonna suspect you? You've never met the guy and you don't have a criminal record."

"But I'm just a writer."

"Yes, but a mystery writer. You think up these murders and then figure out where the killers make their mistakes. Who better to plan the perfect murder than a mystery writer?"

Joe shook his head and looked desperately at his wife. "That's ridiculous. Okay, at least tell me one thing."

"Okay?"

"Out of everyone in New York City, how did you select *me*?"

Pockmarked Cop Face smiled big. "Your lucky day, Joe. I'm told it was almost completely random."

"Why don't you just kill this guy yourself?"

"I represent a party who would love nothing more than to see this man's name in the obituary column. However, for business reasons, we cannot be directly involved with any attempts on his life. So we found you."

"The man you want killed, what does he do?"

"Fuck you care what he does? Your only concern should be getting your daughter home in one piece."

Joe looked at Denise. "What if I die trying to do this thing?"

Pockmarked Cop Face grinned. "You'd better not."

"Or what?"

"We'll kill Emily."

Joe kept his mouth shut, took a moment to collect his thoughts. "Will this man be alone when I go to the hotel?"

"No. He'll be surrounded by more dicks than Jenna Jameson in a gangbang flick."

"And what am I supposed to do about them?"

"Be resourceful."

"What does that mean?"

"Kill anyone who gets in your way."

"When is this supposed to happen?"

"You have a day to prepare. You kill him in two days. It cannot be the next day or the day after. No extenuating circumstances."

"And after I've killed him?"

"You wait by the phone. Once we've confirmed that you've taken him out, you'll receive a call telling you where to pick up your daughter."

"What do I tell the police about Emily? I have to tell them something."

"You tell 'em a bunch of niggers broke in and held you and your wife at gunpoint as they rifled through your belongings. Tell 'em they kidnapped your little girl but didn't say shit about where they were taking her or why."

"They're not gonna believe that."

"Why?"

"Because it sounds like bullshit. What was I supposed to be doing while all of this was happening?"

Pockmarked Cop Face laughed. "Same thing you're doing now. Tell 'em you tried to fight the men off and they shot you in the shoulder."

"What—?"

Before Joe could finish, Pockmarked Cop Face shot him in the shoulder. Joe screamed out, the force of the bullet knocking him back. The pain was excruciating.

"Now, are you clear on what you're supposed to do?"

Joe nodded, holding his bleeding shoulder. "Crystal."

"I want you to know that we're not fucking around."

"I don't think you are."

Pockmarked Cop Face grinned. "I think you do. Before I leave, I'm going to prove to you that we're serious." He paused for a moment. "Here's what you do: When the cops come, you tell them you got shot in the shoulder. Then you tell them the jigs shot your wife in the head and killed her."

In the brief millisecond between Joe's hearing the words and comprehending what they meant, the man raised his pistol to Denise's head. Joe lunged wildly, and again came the hard blow

7

to the back of the head. And in that briefest of moments he saw the man fire a round into the side of Denise's head.

And the world went black.

DAY TWO

Detective Mertis Whitlock sat at his desk, nodding his head to "Tell Me Something Good" on the radio. He absently chewed at the ham-and-cheese loaf sandwich his wife had packed for him, occasionally dipping it in his cup of coffee, and looking at his new partner, Jillian, doing paperwork at an adjacent desk. A cute little white thing, 26 or 27 years old, Mertis briefly considered flirting with her, but thought the better of it. Instead he said, "Something about Joe Gibson's report feels wrong."

Jillian looked up. "Which part?"

"Him saying he doesn't know who killed his wife and took his little girl."

"Yeah? Why?"

"I've been doing this job for a long time, and I can tell when someone's bullshitting me. Gibson was definitely bullshitting me."

"You think Gibson killed his old lady?"

"No, no, nothing like that. I think he's lying about it being four brothers, for one thing."

"Why is that?"

"The perps didn't steal anything," Mertis said. "They just came for the little girl."

"So?"

"In case you haven't noticed, brothers don't kidnap little white girls very often. It's not their M.O. And there's no ransom request. They just came by, popped Mrs. Gibson, and took the little girl? That shit doesn't make sense. Something doesn't add up."

"So what are you saying?"

9

"I think Gibson is full of shit. I think he can ID the guys who did this."

"Why would he lie?"

"Could be one of three reasons, as far as I can figure."

"Which are?"

"One, he's too scared to tell us the truth—afraid these guys might come back after him. Two, maybe he's working out a ransom deal with them in private. Three, maybe he's planning on going after these men on his own."

"He doesn't seem like the revenge type."

"No, he doesn't, which means it's gotta be one of the first two reasons. My gut tells me he's scared."

"Who could blame him?" Jillian asked. "Considering what they did to his wife, it's no wonder the guy is scared."

"No shit."

"So what are you gonna do?"

"I think I'll give him a day or so and stop back in and check on him, maybe try and get some answers."

Joe knocked on the door of his brother Billy's house. Billy wasn't home. He was upstate, serving out the second of a three-year B&E sentence. Today Joe was here to see Roberto, Billy's lover and sometimes partner in crime.

Roberto came to the screen door. Shirtless, with a big Puerto Rican flag tattoo visible on his chest, he opened the door just a crack and looked at Joe suspiciously. "What brings you to Red Hook, Joe?"

"I need some help."

Roberto's eyes narrowed. "We haven't heard from you in two years, man."

"I'm sorry. I've been busy."

"He's your brother. He misses you. You can't take an hour out of your busy schedule to go and visit him?"

"What can I say? I don't like seeing him behind bars."

"No one does. But you don't do it for yourself—you do it for Billy, so he knows we haven't forgotten him."

"You're right. I'll go see him."

Roberto opened the door just a little more. "You look like shit, Joe."

"What can I say? The past day has been pretty shitty."

"Everything okay?"

"Not really, but I don't want to talk about it."

"Fair enough. You said something about needing help?"

"I'm in a situation. I need guns."

Roberto laughed. "Then go to Wal-Mart."

"I'm serious. I need guns that are clean and untraceable."

"What you need guns for?"

"I'm going hunting."

"What kind of animal you hunting?"

"I can't tell you any more, Roberto. It's better for both of us that way."

Roberto nodded. "I'll set you up with a guy I know, he'll get you some guns. But you gotta promise to go see your brother soon."

"I will."

"You promise?"

"Cross my heart."

Joe met Roberto's friend, Bastard—presumably a nickname— at a seedy motel about ten minutes from Billy and Roberto's place. A heavyset black guy, Bastard looked like a defensive lineman. Inside the room, Bastard opened a big metallic case containing six different handguns. He removed each of the pistols, spreading them out on the bed.

Joe looked them over. He knew very little about guns, but two of them stood out, mainly because they looked badass.

Joe pointed to one of them. "May I?"

"Sure."

Joe picked up the big handgun, weighing it in his hand.

"You know anything about guns?" Bastard asked.

"Not a thing."

"That's a Smith & Wesson. They call that model the Governor. It fires either .45 rounds or .410 bore shotshells, your choice. It retails for about $700 new. I'll sell you this one for five bills."

"It's clean?"

Bastard grinned. "All my guns are clean."

"How powerful is this one?"

"The Governor is so powerful it'll drop a bear with a single shot, so just imagine what it would do to some knucklehead motherfucker on the street."

Joe nodded. With the gun still in hand, he pointed at another pistol. "And that one?"

"That there's the Beretta 96A1."

"Is it a .45?"

"Nah, the 96A1 is a .40 caliber handgun."

"As powerful as a .45?"

Bastard laughed. "She can knock a crackhead nigga out his shoes at a hundred feet."

"What does it cost?"

"The Beretta retails for about seven bills. I can sell you this one for $500, as well."

"I'll take 'em both."

DAY THREE

Joe finally nodded off early in the morning two days after the murder of his wife. He only slept for about forty-five minutes, but he slept nonetheless. His head hurt like hell, and he felt dull aches in both his shoulder and his heart. He missed his wife and daughter dearly. Just after waking, Joe allowed himself to cry for the first time since the men had shown up at his home and changed his life forever.

It rained heavily, which perfectly fit Joe's mood. Today would be the day he would kill a complete stranger. Joe recognized the man from the newspapers. Carlo Ventimiglia, an elderly man— some kind of Mafia boss from Chicago. Joe felt sick inside, and had serious doubts that he would survive to see his wife's funeral.

Two hours later, Joe found himself standing in the rain in front of the swanky hotel where Ventimiglia and his goons were staying. According to the file the bastards had left him, the gangster and his entourage had the entire second floor reserved. Joe looked at his watch and saw it was just after ten a.m. Noting a huge Catholic church on the corner, Joe turned and walked in that direction. He didn't consider himself a religious man, but he felt he could use a little religion on this particular day.

He stepped out of the rain and into the church, his heavy black raincoat concealing the two holstered handguns. Just after Joe entered the foyer, his coat dripping water all over the carpet, a young priest approached him. "Can I help you?" the priest asked.

"I'd like to confess my sins."

The priest smiled and said, "No problem," escorting him to the confessional. Joe stepped inside and sat down. The priest climbed into the opposite end of the confessional, speaking through the partition. "How long has it been since your last confession?"

"Forever."

"How long is that?"

"I've never confessed my sins before."

"Are you Catholic?"

"No, Father."

"What religious denomination are you?"

"I have no religious denomination."

"What brings you here today?"

"Special circumstances."

"Which are?"

"I'm about to kill some people, Father."

Joe could hear the shock in the priest's voice. "Excuse me?"

"I'm not happy about it, Father, but I have no choice."

"I see."

"So what do I do now?"

"Well, it's my hope that you might reconsider."

"No, I mean how many Hail Marys do I say?"

Joe entered the Hyperion Hotel just before eleven. According to the information he'd been given, Ventimiglia and his men would be leaving for a meeting at any moment. The hotel had a large lobby filled with seats and assorted plant life. Joe sat down in one of the plush seats, the only person in the lobby. A large baby grand piano sat silently to his left. A large fountain sat in the center of the room, nearly blocking Joe's view of the elevator. He kept to himself, watching the few people who littered the downstairs area of the hotel come and go. Thankfully, none of them looked like mob guys, and none of them seemed to pay him any mind at all.

Joe had been waiting for about ten minutes when the elevator doors opened and Ventimiglia's entourage came pouring out. Surrounded by goons—Joe counted four of them, all dressed in black suits—the feeble old man wore some sort of oxygen mask.

Now was the moment to act.

Do or die time.

Joe reached into his jacket, his right hand curling around the handle of the big Smith & Wesson. His other hand located the handle of the Beretta. He stood up, bringing out the guns in a single fluid motion. He still had not been seen thanks to the fountain.

Too frightened to think about what he was doing, Joe moved on autopilot. If he considered his actions, he would chicken out.

Joe moved to the right of the fountain, his right arm coming up, the Smith & Wesson settling on a target. He squeezed the trigger and the handgun came to life, dropping the gray-haired Mafioso walking just to the right of Ventimiglia. Joe moved his arm slightly to the left and squeezed the trigger again. The mobsters were aware of him now, and they were scrambling in different directions. A fat man to the left of Ventimiglia jumped in front of him, blocking Joe's shot. The bullet, intended for Ventimiglia, tore the man's throat apart.

A gunshot came from behind the old man, but it went wide and missed Joe by more than a foot. Joe fired his third shot. This one struck the old man square in the face. In an instant Ventimiglia was gone, replaced by a faint blood mist.

"*They hit the boss!*" someone yelled.

Another shot rang out. Joe heard it strike the piano behind him. Joe swiveled slightly, the Smith & Wesson settling on another target. Shot number four struck a retreating mobster in the back of the head, his brains coming to rest on the wall before him.

Only one man left now.

Joe's body moved on instinct. He wasn't aware of it, but every one of his shots had hit a target—and at a distance. This would have been considered exceptional shooting for a professional, but for a novice it was more like a miracle.

The last mobster tried to keep the fountain between Joe and himself. Joe moved to his right and popped off another shot, this one tearing into the metal elevator doors. Joe moved slowly toward the fountain, the Smith & Wesson still raised in his right hand. After a moment of silence, the guy ran out from behind the fountain to Joe's right. The man had a pistol in each hand, firing them both as he ran. Shots zinged off the walls and floor to Joe's left and right, but none of them touched him.

Joe squeezed the trigger and popped off the Smith & Wesson's last round. The bullet struck the guy in the chin and he dropped to the tile floor. As Joe moved toward him, he could see the man was still alive. He had fallen on his face and now tried to crawl. Joe holstered the Smith & Wesson and grabbed the Beretta with his right hand. Two feet from the wounded mobster, Joe raised the Beretta, aiming it at the top of the man's head. He squeezed the trigger and the man stopped crawling.

Joe looked over the bodies to make sure everyone was dead. Convinced they were, he started to turn. Just as he did, he saw one of them—the fat one with the torn-out throat—move his arm slightly. Joe raised the Beretta and fired a shot through the man's head.

On the way out of the hotel, Joe looked over at the two desk clerks—one male, one female—peeking over the top of the counter. He raised the Beretta in their direction and they disappeared beneath the counter once more.

Joe strolled out of the hotel nonchalantly, holding the front door open for an elderly woman entering the building.

Mertis Whitlock pulled the Crown Vic into Joe Gibson's driveway. He crushed out his cigarette in the ashtray and turned off the engine. The rain fell harder now than it had when he left the station, and he now wished he'd thought to bring an umbrella. He climbed out of the car, pulling the top of his raincoat up over his head, and ran toward the house. He raced up the steps and onto the front porch. He pulled the raincoat back down and rang the doorbell.

No one answered.

"Shit," he said to himself. He turned and looked around at the quiet neighborhood. Not wanting to battle the rain again any time soon, Mertis decided he'd stick around for a few minutes and wait for Gibson. He reached into his coat pocket and fished out the pack of smokes. He slid a cigarette out of the pack and put it to his lips. Letting it dangle there, he lit it.

After smoking two more cigarettes and having waited for about fifteen minutes, Mertis decided it was time to give up and head back to the station. Just as he came to this conclusion, he saw Joe Gibson's blue Ford Expedition coming down the street. Since Mertis had parked in the driveway, blocking the garage, Gibson parked along the curb in front of the house.

A moment later Gibson joined Mertis on the front porch. Mertis saw that Gibson was not wearing a coat. "Helluva day to leave your coat at home."

Gibson laughed halfheartedly. "I've had a lot on my mind."

"Makes sense."

"So what brings you out in this weather, detective?"

"I just wanted to ask you a few more questions."

Gibson nodded, but didn't seem to care one way or the other. He looked up at Mertis, lighting another cigarette. "Can you spare one of those?"

Mertis held out the pack. "You smoke?"

17

"I haven't smoked in a long time. Maybe seven, eight years. But now..."

Mertis nodded. There was nothing more to say.

Gibson put the cigarette in his mouth, and Mertis lit it.

"Your face is looking a little better," Mertis said.

Gibson rubbed his jaw. "Still hurts like hell, though."

"I'd imagine. And the shoulder?"

"Ditto. So what was it you wanted to ask me?"

"Look, Mr. Gibson, I know you're probably scared, and you know, you've got good reason to be frightened. But the men who shot your wife and kidnapped your little girl—"

"Yes?"

"Are you absolutely sure you can't ID them?"

"I told you, there were four black guys. They—"

Gibson was interrupted by Mertis's cell phone, now ringing. "Hold on a sec," Mertis said, answering the phone.

"Hello?"

Mertis listened for a moment before saying, "At the Hyperion Hotel? I'll be right there."

He closed the phone and looked at Gibson. "I'm afraid I've gotta go. Duty calls."

Gibson put his hand out and Mertis shook it.

"I may come back around in a day or so," Mertis said. "Do you still have my card?"

"Yeah."

"Good. If you think of anything else, you give me a call. Okay?"

"Sure thing."

Mertis turned and prepared to run back into the rain, but Gibson stopped him. "Detective?"

"Yeah?"

"You think I could bum one more smoke from you?"

DAYS FOUR AND FIVE

A hell of a day for an outdoor funeral. The unrelenting rain came down from the slate gray sky. Joe sat front and center under the funeral canopy, Denise's closed coffin about a foot in front of him. Joe could feel the crowd's gaze upon him, all of them wanting to see him cry. But Joe had no tears. He was in a dark place so black it transcended tears and self-pity.

He could hear the minister droning on and on, reciting that old chestnut from Ecclesiastes about there being a time for everything under heaven. Joe had just been a million miles away from here, somewhere deep inside his own mind. But now he was back. He'd never had much use for religion and he'd never seen the Bible as being anything more than a collection of poetry and fairy tales, but the line about there being a time to die pushed a button.

What a crock of shit this was.

It hadn't been Denise's time to die at all, and any God who believed otherwise could be nothing more than a self-serving asshole. She was only thirty-five; she should have had her whole life in front of her. And here was this jerk-off minister—a man who'd never even met his agnostic wife—saying it was her time to die, as if that made everything better. And what did the minister care? He probably had five more of these things lined up for today. This, for him, was just another job, one as impersonal as the next.

"A time to be silent, and a time to speak," the minster said.

Joe didn't plan it, but he felt himself stand up.

He heard a few gasps behind him. The minister stopped speaking and stared at him, unsure how best to proceed.

Joe looked him in the eyes. "I'm sorry, but this all bullshit."

19

Joe turned and walked out into the rain.

Joe waited patiently for the kidnappers' call, but it did not come. He wanted to pass the time, but nothing seemed relevant anymore. What, was he gonna sit and read a book while his wife moldered in the ground and his daughter was God knows where? Could he possibly be expected to sit and watch today's episode of *Jeopardy* and actually give a fuck about any of it? The world had lost meaning for him. With Emily's return, there was a slight chance he might find some shred of meaning once again, but for now there was nothing.

A few days before, he'd been roughly halfway through a new novel. He'd been on a tear lately, and the damned thing had just seemed to write itself. Joe believed it to be the best thing he'd ever written, which he found sad considering he knew he would never finish it. Maybe one day he would feel like writing again, but not on that particular book. No, that project would forever serve as a reminder of a life and time that no longer existed.

Joe sat on the front porch steps, chain-smoking Pall Malls and drinking Maker's Mark from the bottle, the telephone sitting on his lap. He stared at the dark sky, but found no answers. He looked around the quiet neighborhood through a veil of rain, his wounded shoulder aching.

It had now been almost two days and he hadn't heard from the kidnappers. Surely they knew by now Ventimiglia was dead. It was all over the news. How could they not? And now a different realization began to settle in—perhaps Joe had killed all those men for nothing. At this point, it didn't feel like much of a stretch to assume that Emily wasn't coming home.

The bottle of Maker's Mark went dry just before dark. Feeling drunk and lost in despair, Joe passed out on the porch.

The rain continued to fall.

And the phone refused to ring.

After waking the next morning and discovering the kidnappers still hadn't called, Joe decided to pay his brother Billy a visit in prison. Visitation wasn't as bad as he expected. Rather than using telephones to talk to one another through a glass window, Joe and Billy were allowed to sit across from each other at a table. Other families visited at tables all around them. The screams of babies drowned out virtually all other sounds, and the stench of their piss-filled diapers hung heavily in the room.

"What's a nice guy like you doing in a place like this?" Billy asked, grinning.

"What, I can't visit my brother?"

"I guess there's a first for everything."

"I guess so."

"You look like shit."

"Funny, I feel like shit."

"Write any good books lately?"

"Not according to the critics."

"Yeah, the guy in the *Times* said *Everybody Loses* was derivative of your earlier work."

"Yeah, well, fuck him. What does he know?"

"Right."

"The reason I'm here—a group of men broke into my house. They murdered Denise."

Billy's eyes got big and he sat forward. *"What?"*

"And they kidnapped Emily."

"The baby?"

"Well, she's hardly a baby anymore. She's eight now."

"They asking for a ransom?"

"No."

"Damn. That's fucked up. The cops got any leads?"

"Fuck the cops. I'm gonna take care of this myself."

Billy looked around to make sure no one was listening. "You sure that's a good idea?"

"It is what it is."

"You need some help? I could get Roberto to help you out."

"I'm good. I need to do this one myself."

"Be careful, bro."

"The reason I'm here—I need your help."

"Anything," Billy said. "What can I do?"

"I'm trying to locate the men who did this." Joe then described each of the men in full detail. Billy could only be sure about the Mexican, the most distinctive of the bunch.

"His name's Hector. Hector Carrera. They call him Gonzo, like on *The Muppet Show*? He's a small-time hood, does B&Es, works as a heavy, sometimes a hitter. Last I knew he was doing a stretch up in Sing Sing. I guess he's out now. I'll call Roberto, find out where Hector's staying. Roberto'll call you tomorrow."

"What else can you tell me about this guy?"

"I pulled a couple jobs with him a few years back. We weren't partners, exactly—we were part of a team. But this fuckin' guy, this asshole Hector, fucked everything up the last time we worked together. I almost got my head blown off because of him."

"Anything else you can tell me about him?"

"You don't fuck around with a guy like Hector. You make one mistake and you're dead."

DAY SIX

Hector lived in the Meat Packing District, and not in those fancy new apartments like they show on *Sex and the City*. Hector's dilapidated piece of shit house was the last one standing on his block, and it was doozie. Joe couldn't understand how the rat trap hadn't been condemned yet.

It was a few minutes before four in the afternoon when Joe drove by, checking out the place. He saw no sign of the big Mexican, but a great big motorcycle with a naked woman and flames painted on its tank was parked beside the porch. Joe figured it had to be Hector's.

Joe parked the Expedition a block down the street. This time he left the holsters in the truck, instead carrying the pistols in the front pockets of his slacks. With no prior experience, he wasn't very good at any of this, but he figured he would just walk right up to the door and knock. Then, when Hector answered, there would be hell to pay. When Joe got to the house, he walked quietly up the creaky steps and onto the even creakier porch. He slid the pistols from his pockets, and banged on the wooden door.

A dog started barking from somewhere inside the shack, and Joe could hear a man saying "fucking hold on a minute." About thirty seconds later, the door swung open.

And there was Hector—the same bastard who'd helped hold he and his wife captive.

One of the bastards who'd shot Denise and taken Emily.

Hector wore ratty jeans and no shirt, sloppy prison tattoos all over his chest and abdomen.

Joe raised both arms, the pistols aimed at Hector.

"You?" Hector said. "Fuck do you want?"

23

"What do you think I want?"

"If I knew, I wouldn't have asked."

Joe moved forward, making his way through the door. Once his arms were inside the door frame, Hector slammed the door shut against them, causing Joe to drop the pistols. *"Arrrggghh,"* Joe managed, sliding to the ground. Before Joe knew what was happening, he felt Hector's boot kicking him in the side of the head. Joe fell hard. As he did, Hector picked up the Smith & Wesson.

Hector chuckled, looking down the block to make sure there were no witnesses.

"Get up, asshole."

Joe rubbed his head before climbing slowly to his feet. Now his wounded shoulder, his arms, and his head all hurt like a sonofabitch.

Hector stood over him, motioning for him to go inside. Joe did. Inside, the strong stench of dog shit was overpowering. Trash piles towered everywhere, and the remnants of TV dinners past were lying all around.

Joe did not want to die here amongst all this garbage with that damned dog still barking somewhere in the house.

"I love what you've done with the place," Joe said.

"You think because you got a nice house and you some kind of big shot writer that your shit don't stink?"

"Not as bad as your house does."

Hector laughed again. There was a finality in his laughter this time, and Joe knew he would die soon unless he did something quickly.

"Sit down," Hector said, motioning toward a green recliner that looked like it had been purchased in 1976.

Joe did as he was told.

Hector raised the Smith & Wesson, aiming it directly into Joe's face.

"Got any last words, *puta*?"

Joe said nothing.

He watched Hector's finger tense. He pulled the trigger.

Nothing happened.

Joe had forgotten to switch off the safety!

A brief expression of confusion flashed across Hector's face. He turned the handgun sideways to inspect it, and Joe kicked him in the balls as hard as he could. Hector let out a squeal like an injured cat. He fell backwards, but managed to keep the gun in hand. Before he could get to the safety, Joe was on him again, kicking him in the side of the head.

He kicked him again.

And again.

And again.

Hector no longer moved, his eyes closed. Certain he'd killed the big Mexican, Joe took a moment to catch his breath. Then heard Hector laughing again. Joe looked up, noticed the huge, gaudy orange lamp—another holdover from the Seventies—and grabbed it. He held it over his head just as Hector switched off the safety, and he brought the lamp down as hard as he could onto the injured man's face.

This time Hector lost consciousness.

Joe retrieved the Smith & Wesson. He climbed onto Hector's chest, straddling him, the pistol right in the man's face. He slapped Hector's cheek to revive him. This did the trick and Hector opened his eyes groggily.

"What the fuck, man?"

"I need answers."

"Not from me."

Joe cocked back the hammer.

"We killed your wife—you gonna kill me no matter what I say, right?" Hector said.

"Maybe, maybe not. You tell me what I wanna know, you just might make it out of here in a wheelchair or a coma. You don't, the only way you leave here is in a fucking body bag."

Hector chuckled. "Tha's good, the part about the wheelchair or the coma. You pretty good at this, Mr. Gibson. In another life, you coulda been me."

"I don't think so."

Hector's expression turned angry. "Why? You too good to be me?"

"Cockroaches are too good to be you."

Hector grinned. "Tha's a good one."

Joe repositioned the pistol in Hector's face. "Where's Emily?"

"Who's Emily?"

"My daughter."

"Oh," Hector said, a look of recognition washing over his face. "The little girl."

"Where the fuck is she?"

"I heard you killed that grease-ball Ventimiglia at that hotel. That was you, right?"

Joe nodded.

"And they didn't give you your little girl back?"

"No."

"Tha's fucked up." Joe read Hector's expression to be a sincere one.

Joe's eyes narrowed. "You telling me you don't know what they did with my daughter?"

"Man, I didn't know shit about the little girl. I didn't even know they was gonna shoot your old lady. They didn't tell me any of that shit. It was just a job, man. I ain't got nothing against you. It was, you know, just a job. It wasn't personal."

"It was pretty fucking personal to me."

"I guess, but man, you gotta understand how this kind of shit works."

"Explain it to me."

"I got a call."

"Who called you?"

"My man Jonesy."

"Was he one of the guys with you that night?"

The look on Hector's face made it apparent that he'd said more than he wanted to.

Joe pushed the barrel of the Smith & Wesson against Hector's nose. "I said, was Jonesy there that night?"

"Yeah."

"Which one was he?"

"The nigger with the fucked up hair, look like a skinny Don King?"

"He was the one who called you?"

"Yeah."

"So he put this thing together?"

"No, he didn't tell me who put it all together. He was just a hired hand like me. He said it was a need-to-know-basis kind of thing and if I needed to know, then I didn't need the job. I said, 'Shit, I need the work. My dumb ass ain't gotta know nothing about nothing,' you know?"

"Did you know any of the other guys who were there?"

"One of 'em, the white guy who looked like a cop?"

"Yeah?"

"I saw him around when I was in Lewisburg a few years back. He hung out with the Aryans."

"You know his name?"

Hector shook his head. "I didn't associate with those guys."

"Are you sure you don't know who orchestrated this thing?"

"I'm sure, man. Scout's fucking honor."

"Do you know how or why they picked me?"

"No fucking clue. The white guy said something about it being random, but tha's all I really know."

"You don't know shit."

"No, man, I'm telling you."

"Why did they want Ventimiglia dead?"

"I dunno that either. Shit, man, I don't even know who I was working for."

Joe took a moment to collect his thoughts. Finally, he said, "Okay, how do I get ahold of Jonesy?"

Hector smiled. "No way, man. You ain't gettin' shit outta me."

"You sure about that?"

"Definitely."

Joe moved the Smith & Wesson, shooting Hector in the left shoulder. Hector wailed for a moment, but then went quiet. He was breathing hard. "Looks like no wheelchair or coma for me, man, because I ain't tellin' you shit. You gon' hafta kill me."

"This is your last chance, Hector."

Hector spat at Joe's face, but none of the spittle reached him.

Joe pulled the trigger and fired a round directly through Hector's dead white eye.

"Fuck, Hector, you coulda just told me what I needed to know."

As Joe took a deep breath of air, he glanced over at the table beside him where the orange lamp had been. There was a tattered Southwestern Bell phone book sitting there, a few names scrawled on its cover. Joe picked it up and looked at it. One of the names was Jonesy, a Brooklyn address written just beneath it. Joe tore off the phone book cover and stuck it in his pocket.

He retrieved the Beretta from the floor by the door. Joe wanted to do one more thing before he left. He followed the sound of the barking dog back into the kitchen, where he found a bruised and battered, half-starved Rottweiler locked in a cage. He opened the cage and let the sickly animal go free. The Rottweiler then went immediately to its fallen owner and started sniffing his body. The dog hiked up his back leg and pissed in Hector's face.

DAY SEVEN: PART ONE

Mertis and Jillian examined the lobby of the Hyperion Hotel again. Mertis stood in the same place Joe Gibson had been standing four days before. He had his arms raised outward, fingers pointed like guns, reenacting the shootout the way he figured it went down. Jillian was looking at the bullet hole in the piano a few feet away.

Mertis was firing imaginary rounds. *"Bam! Bam!* Then the shooter apparently ran out of bullets in the Smith & Wesson and switched guns. He then moved in to finish them off at point blank range with the Beretta."

"I read this the same way you do," Jillian said. "There had to be two shooters."

"Otherwise it doesn't make sense. Why would the shooter fire two shots from the Beretta and then switch handguns again before popping the two desk clerks and the old lady?"

"Right, the Glock nine."

Mertis looked at the front desk. "For a job like this, you need a second man for crowd control. I'd bet you dollars to doughnuts he's the guy removed the surveillance tapes. The primary shooter wouldn't have had time for all that."

"And the way the desk clerks and the old woman were shot—"

"Execution-style."

"Those shootings seem inconsistent with the others."

"I can't put my finger on it, but something about the five wiseguys by the elevator feels funny, like the shooter was an amateur."

"His shots were pretty consistent for an amateur."

"Mighta been dumb luck. Thing is, this doesn't feel like a mob hit at all. Usually in a mob hit, the targets are taken out at close range so there's no chance of anyone escaping."

"So you think it was amateur night?"

"These guys, yes," Mertis said, pointing at the elevator area. He turned and motioned toward the front desk. "But those shootings—the desk clerks and the old woman—were done by a pro. But why would a pro sit back and watch the amateur gun down all the wiseguys by himself? It doesn't make sense."

"What are you thinking?"

Mertis bit his lip. "I'm thinking how odd it is that Denise Gibson gets murdered execution-style, and then three days later we have more execution-style murders here at the hotel. I also find it odd that we had what is possibly a group of pros there to take out Mrs. Gibson—a civilian—and then an amateur here to take out a Mafia boss. None of it makes a damned bit of sense."

"What does your gut say?"

"I think the two cases might be connected."

"How so?"

"I don't know yet. I'm still trying to connect the dots."

Joe took a shower, hot water cascading down over his body, making him feel just the tiniest bit better for the briefest of moments. He hadn't slept more than a few hours in the six days following Denise's death, and it was starting to catch up with him. His head hurt like hell and he felt weak.

Joe had shaving cream all over his face. He had just begun shaving, and had removed only a single row of the cream, when a voice spoke to him from outside the shower curtain. "Turn off the water and get out. And don't try any bullshit or I'll shoot you."

What the hell?

Who could this be?

Joe didn't recognize the voice. He turned off the water and slowly pulled back the shower curtain. There was a man standing there with a Glock nine aimed right in his face. The guy was Italian, probably about thirty, had jet black hair with a goatee, and wore a black suit just like the men Joe had killed in the lobby of the Hyperion Hotel. He was definitely a wiseguy, probably one of Ventimiglia's. If that was the case, Joe was as good as dead.

"Who are you?" Joe asked.

"I'm sure you've got a pretty good idea. We'll talk about that. We've got time. First things first, why don't you cover yourself with a towel or something? It's hard talking business with a guy who's got his dick hanging out."

Joe looked down and realized he was completely naked. He grabbed the towel hanging over the curtain rod and pulled it down, wrapping it around his waist.

"Okay, so who are you?"

The man smiled. "How about I tell you my last name and you tell me if that rings any bells."

"Okay."

"Ventimiglia."

Joe tried to play it cool. "That supposed to mean something to me?"

"Look, you can't bullshit me, because I already know you killed my uncle and all those other fucks in that hotel."

"What makes you think so?"

"Because you left the surveillance videos in the machine, Einstein. If I hadn't taken those tapes and killed the desk clerks, you'd be in jail already."

"Why'd you save my ass?"

"I didn't do it for you," the man said. "It's my job to track you down. If you end up in jail, then I'm not gonna be able to catch you."

"Are you gonna kill me?"

"We'll get to that. Now you're obviously not a criminal mastermind, so I wanna know why you killed those guys."

"Four men broke into my house last week and took my wife and I at gunpoint," Joe said. "They demanded that I murder your uncle."

The man cocked his head. "Why *you*?"

"No one ever gave me a good reason. They said it was 'almost random.'"

"Who were they working for?"

"I don't know yet."

The man nodded, taking this in. "Go on."

"They murdered my wife and kidnapped my eight-year-old daughter."

"So you go and kill Carlo and those other guys to get your daughter back?"

"Yeah. Only thing is, they never gave back my daughter."

"Really? You do all that, and you don't get your daughter back?"

"Right."

"That's fucked up. So what do you do? Call the cops?"

"I can't go to the cops. I mean, I killed a bunch of people. So I've been tracking these men down myself."

"And?"

"I've located two of them so far."

"And you've met with them?"

"I met with the first one."

"How did that go?"

"He's dead now."

"You killed him?"

"He didn't die of old age."

The man nodded. "You gettin' pretty good at this killing thing, Joe. So what about the second guy?"

"I was gonna visit him today."

"That puts us in an awkward position," the man said.

"How's that?"

"Because I'm here to kill you now."

Joe thought about it, and to his surprise, realized he really didn't care all that much. Without Denise and Emily in his life—and there was a good chance he'd never see Emily again—he had nothing to live for. "Tell you what, how about you wait a couple days and you let me talk to these people—"

"By talk you mean kill."

"Semantics."

"And then what?"

"You let me finish what I started and then you kill me when I'm done."

The man nodded. "I could help you track down these guys and get to the bottom of all this. Then I could find out who's responsible for killing my uncle Carlo." He looked up at Joe. "Besides you, I mean."

Joe shrugged. "Sorry. It wasn't personal. I didn't even know the guy."

"It's okay. He was a hard-on anyway."

"Yeah?"

"Yeah, so don't worry about it," the man said. "I'm gonna have to kill you either way. I mean, an example has to be made, but Carlo was no big loss to me."

"Good. So we've got a deal."

"Yeah, we got a deal."

Joe put his hand out for the man to shake, but the man declined. "You're still naked under that towel, my friend. I ain't shakin' hands with no naked guys."

After Joe got dressed, he and Carlo Ventimiglia's nephew sat down at the table and drank coffee with whiskey and downed a few Eggo waffles with maple syrup.

"We gotta lay down some ground rules if we're gonna do this," the man said.

"Okay, you name 'em."

"Rule number one is you don't try to get cocky and either take a shot at me or try to escape. You do either one of those things, you're gonna be as dead as Michael Jackson. Second rule, you don't try to be my long lost buddy. No matter how friendly we get, I'm still gonna kill you when this is all said and done. *Capice?*"

"That it? Those are the rules?"

The man stared at him. "There will be more rules to come. I think of any more, I'll pass 'em along."

"Fair enough," Joe said. "So what do I call you?"

"Sir, if you're smart."

"No, seriously. What's your name?"

"I guess it can't hurt to tell you my name. Who are you gonna tell? It's Vinnie."

"Vinnie, I got a rule for you."

Vinnie couldn't believe his ears. "Really? *You* got a rule for *me?*"

"Yeah."

"Okay, let's hear it."

"Tracking down these assholes is my thing, not yours. So when we go busting down these fuckers' doors, I lead the way. It's my show. I do the talking."

Vinnie thought about it for a minute. "Okay, what the hell. Sure, it's your show." He ate a big mouthful of waffles before speaking again. "But I got another rule, too. From now on, we take my car. You ride shotgun."

DAY SEVEN: PART TWO

Jonesy's apartment sat atop a dusty, junk-filled pawn shop. Joe and Vinnie took the stairs, guns out, and were surprised to find a note on Jonesy's door that read: "COME ON IN, SWEET THING. DOOR'S UNLOCKED." Vinnie smirked at Joe and said, "I don't think this note's for us." Vinnie took the note down and crumpled it, dropping it to the floor.

Joe opened the door, gun still out, prepared for whatever. Inside he discovered a clean, well-decorated apartment with scented candles lit all around. The scents of baked apple pie, vanilla, coffee, cookies, and probably a dozen other aromas combined with burning incense to create a smoky smell that was at once welcoming and sickening. Some light old-school R&B song—Joe thought it might be Teddy Pendergrass—filled the room.

Jonesy was nowhere to be seen.

Joe led the way through the apartment. He turned a corner and found Jonesy sitting at table, dressed only in a fluffy pink robe and a black do-rag, snorting cocaine through a ceramic straw from a small mirror. Jonesy looked up, eyes watering, and saw the two white men standing there with their guns out. "What the fuck?"

Vinnie grinned. "And you must be Mr. Jonesy, I presume?"

Jonesy didn't pay much attention to Vinnie. Instead he stared at Joe uneasily, either recognizing him and wondering why the fuck he was here, or wondering exactly where he'd seen him before.

"You're Gibson," Jonesy said, pointing the ceramic straw at him. "The writer."

35

"And you're the fuckhead who helped kill my wife and kidnap my little girl."

Jonesy started to get defensive. "Look, that shit wasn't me."

"You telling me you weren't there at my house six days ago? You telling me it was some other skinny asshole with a big fucked-up Don King hairdo was there and not you?"

"Nah, of course not. I'm saying I ain't have shit to do with any of that. That wasn't my thing. I was just there on a job, nothing more. The man called and said he needed me to go along and harass some guy and his old lady, said he'd pay me two thousand in cash to stand there and act tough. So that's exactly what I did."

"You don't look so tough to me," Vinnie said, prodding the guy. "You got a friggin' pink bath robe, for Chrissakes."

Jonesy looked irritated. "You ain't got no style, man. This shit is in right now."

Vinnie laughed. "Bullshit. Even Rick James wouldn't have been caught dead in that shit, and that was during disco. Hell, pimps wouldn't even wear a get-up like that."

Jonesy started to disagree. Joe straightened his arm, pointing the Smith & Wesson in Jonesy's face, letting him know he meant business. "Who called you about the job?"

"White guy by the name of Nicky Needles. He was there, at your house."

"Was he the skinny one or the one with all the pockmarks on his face?"

"The skinny, cheese-eatin' little bastard, look like a rat or somethin'."

"Who was he working for?"

"He didn't say."

"You did the job and didn't know who you were working for?"

"I get a lot of jobs like that."

"And you don't ask?"

"The streets don't work like that, homie. My need for money outweighs my need to know who the fuck is hiring me. At the end of the day, I don't give two shits who's behind the job just as long as my black ass gets paid."

"Did you know either of the other two guys who were there that night?"

Jonesy nodded. "Sure. Hector, big Mexican goes by the name Gonzo? We go way back. We did a stretch together at Lewisburg."

"I'll bet you two were lovers," Vinnie said.

Joe ignored this. "The other white guy—the one who shot my wife? He was in Lewisburg, too. Right?"

"Yeah, he was there. Ran with the Aryans, sold dope. But I didn't know the guy. Just used to see him around. Looked like an asshole. Something about him... He looks like a cop to me, and I don't hang around Aryans or cops."

"What's the guy's name?" Joe asked.

"Damned if I know. He was just another silly-ass white boy to me." Jonesy looked up at Vinnie, squinting his eyes, trying to look tough. "And all y'all ofay motherfuckers look alike to me."

Vinnie grinned. "You're a funny guy, huh?" He reached back and backhanded him with the Glock, leaving Jonesy's nose and mouth bloodied.

Jonesy looked up at Vinnie. "Who the fuck you supposed to be, anyway?"

"I'm Mr. Gibson's attorney," Vinnie said. "I represent Mr. Gibson in such matters as these."

Jonesy smiled. "You gonna serve me with some papers, take me to court?"

Vinnie nodded. "Something like that."

"Maybe I need a lawyer like you."

"You won't after today." Vinnie winked.

Joe broke up this exchange. "Do you know where they took my little girl?"

"Nah, man, I don't. I didn't even see the little girl. I was driving when we went to the bus stop. I know they put her in the trunk, but that's all I know."

"Why would they want to keep my little girl?"

"They *kept* her?" Jonesy asked. "I didn't even know that. I figured when you capped that old linguine-eating greaseball they'd give you your kid back. That's fucked up."

Vinnie nodded in agreement. "Gives honest criminals a bad name."

"Do you have any idea what they would want with a little girl?" Joe asked.

"Hate to break this to you," Jonesy said, "but there are people who would buy a little girl like that. There are places on the other side of the border where dirty old men would pay good money for a little piece of white tail like hers."

Joe was shaken, didn't move.

Vinnie stuck the Glock right up against Jonesy's nose. "You think you could be a little more tactful, asshole?"

"I'm sorry," Jonesy said. "I thought you wanted the truth. Next time I'll just tell you some lies."

Joe said, "Tell me about Nicky Needles."

"What you wanna know?"

"Anything and everything."

"He's an asshole," Jonesy said. "I can't stand that dude. And he's got bad breath, smells like he been eatin' cat shit. I've worked with him a couple of times now, and it's always the same. Dude thinks he knows everything about everything and he can't wait to tell you 'bout it. It's like, 'If you so smart, man, why the fuck you been to prison so many times?'"

"Any idea why he went to prison?" Joe asked.

"Shit," Jonesy said, "which time? Nicky Needles been to prison more times than Carmen Electra's had rock star dick in her. I think the last time he went upstate was for cars. Apparently he was part of some big auto theft ring across the bridge. Another time he got caught with a truck full of stolen merchandise. Furniture, I think. Love seats and ottomans. And they say he went up for rape once—an old woman, I think. Someone's grandma. At least that's the talk around the campfire."

Joe nodded. "Any idea who might employ a guy like that?"

"A guy like Nicky Needles? He works for anyone who'll have his dumbass. I sincerely doubt anyone's got him locked down full time. A guy like that, he's a freelancer all the way. But you find that other guy—the cop-lookin' motherfucker with all the bumps on his face? I'd bet you two blowjobs and a partridge in a fuckin' pear tree he's connected with somebody. You see how he handled shit that night? He just kind of took over, let it be known he was runnin' the show. And who was it that shot your old lady? That same cop-lookin' motherfucker. I'm telling you, you catch him and make him talk, you find out who planned that job."

"I guess we're done with you then," Vinnie said. "No reason to keep you alive now, is there?"

"Look, man," Jonesy said, "I'm telling you, I didn't have nothin' to do with any of that crazy shit happened that night. My black ass was just there to get paid, end of story. They didn't tell me nothin' about no kids, and they damned sure didn't tell me they were planning on murdering someone. I'm on parole. I don't need to be mixed up with no stupid shit like that. Besides all that, now I got you two crazy-looking peckerwoods standing here pointing guns in my face."

Joe smiled at this. "You don't enjoy this?"

"Hell no, I don't like it. To tell you the truth, all this drama is making me a little sick to my stomach."

Vinnie opened his mouth and started to talk some more shit, but the girl walked in. She was young, white, dressed in skimpy clothes with so much eyeliner on that she looked like a raccoon, and scared out of her drugged-out mind. "What the hell is this?" she asked, a stupid, confused look plastered across her pierced-up face.

Joe aimed the Smith & Wesson at her. "And you must be Sweet Thing."

She still looked confused. "What?"

"What's your name?" Vinnie asked.

Sweet Thing said nothing.

Now Vinnie had his Glock aimed at her face. *"I asked you what the fuck your name was, princess."*

"Traci."

Joe turned back to Jonesy. "What if I do to her what you sons of bitches did to my wife?"

Jonesy shrugged. "Fuck do I care? I don't even know this junkie bitch. I met her at the taco stand."

Traci wasn't listening. She could have been a million miles away. Stoned, transfixed by the lines of coke in front of Jonesy.

"Musta been quite a date you had planned here," Vinnie said. "What was on the agenda? A little date rape, a little cocaine?"

"We were gonna shoot some smack and watch *New Jack City* on cable," Jonesy said. "Then later, maybe have some sex. But not until after *New Jack City*. Wesley Snipes is my man in that shit."

Vinnie ignored the Wesley Snipes talk. "You got smack, huh? Of course. I mean, you can't have coke without a little smack, too."

Joe asked, "Where's the heroin?"

Traci snapped out of her trance. "It's in my purse."

"Well, get it out," Vinnie said. "Let's see it."

Traci took out a syringe, a bent spoon, and a baggy filled with powder, sitting them on the table beside Jonesy's coke.

Joe repositioned the Smith & Wesson against Jonesy's face, bending the tip of his nose a little. "I need to know how to get ahold of Nicky Needles."

"You ain't got to put that gun all in my face, man. I don't give a damn about no Nicky fucking Needles. I'll give you that information without the gun, partner. That creepy little bastard hangs out at a bar in the Bronx. It's called The Rabid Rabbit. It's a real dive—nothing but crazy-assed crackers and outlaw country songs about lynchin' niggers and whatnot."

"They make country songs about lynchin' niggers?" Vinnie asked, completely serious.

"How the fuck do I know? All that shit sounds alike to me. I hear that shit, I know it's not for me, the man talkin' about pickup trucks and drinkin' Old Milwaukee."

Joe spoke. "You sure he's gonna be there?"

"Unless he's in prison, which he's apt to be any day now, he'll be in that dingy little shithole. I think he may have some sort of deal going with the owner, like maybe he's getting a percentage of the till or something. I dunno, but he's *always* there. It's like his office."

Joe looked at Vinnie and Vinnie nodded. Joe picked up the syringe. "I'll cook you up a batch of heroin," Joe said, turning and leaving the room.

Vinnie pressed the Glock to Jonesy's temple. "I want you to snort another line of that coke."

Jonesy looked up incredulously. *"Really?"*

"Yeah."

Jonesy grinned. "You ain't got to tell a nigga twice."

Jonesy leaned forward, putting the ceramic straw up to his nose, and started snorting up a line of coke. Jonesy was halfway through the line when Vinnie smashed his head forward against

41

the table, the ceramic straw jamming up his nose. Jonesy started screaming and thrashing around, blood pouring from his nose.

Joe returned from another part of the apartment, holding up the syringe. "Hold his arm steady," Joe said. Vinnie grabbed Jonesy's arm—Jonesy still thrashing around—and pulled up the sleeve of the robe. Joe injected the syringe's contents into Jonesy's vein. Within seconds Jonesy thrashed around even harder than before. He fell to the floor, thrashed around some more, and then went silent.

"What did you inject him with?" Vinnie asked.

"Drain cleaner."

Vinnie laughed.

Traci started freaking out. "You *killed* him?"

Joe nodded, a smile on his lips. "Yeah."

Traci looked at Jonesy's body. "You sure he's dead?"

"He ain't sleeping."

Vinnie pointed the Glock in Traci's face. "I'm sorry to do this, but this is a classic case of you being in the wrong place at the wrong time."

Her eyes got big. "You're gonna shoot me?"

"Unless you want my friend Joe to serve you up one of those drain cleaner cocktails."

"Please don't," Traci begged.

Joe thought of Emily. He looked at Vinnie. "Why don't we let Traci go," he said. "She doesn't even know this guy. I'm sure if we let her go she'll keep her mouth closed about what she saw here."

"That's right," Traci said. "I won't say shit to anybody."

Vinnie shrugged. "You're a lucky girl, Traci. If it was just me, you'd be dead already."

"What are you saying?"

"I'm saying you better start running, and you'd better not stop until you get home. *Capice*?"

And Traci was gone.

DAY SEVEN: PART THREE

True to Jonesy's word, The Rabid Rabbit was a dark, smoke-filled shithole. The place smelled of cheap cigarettes, stale beer, and body odor. The clientele, what little came out in the afternoon, looked like something out of *Deliverance*. The jukebox—a vintage model that still played records—played a tune by David Allan Coe called "My Wife Ran Off with a Nigger."

As Joe and Vinnie were walking in, Vinnie heard a few lines of the song. "Well, what do you know? Jonesy was right. They really do sing songs like that."

Joe scanned the place, searching for Nicky Needles, but saw no sign of the Ichabod Crane-looking motherfucker. As Joe and Vinnie made their way toward the bar, Vinnie spoke again. "I think we're a little out of place here. I think the two of us have more teeth than all of these sons of bitches combined."

A mean-looking fat man with pork chop sideburns, a graying flat-top haircut, and a leather vest eyeballed them from behind the bar. "You boys lost?"

Vinnie and Joe looked at each other. "We're looking for an associate of yours," Vinnie said. "Guy by the name of Nicky Needles."

The bartender looked at them like they were cops. "You two friends of his?"

"What makes you say that?" Vinnie asked. "Do we look like a couple of assholes?"

The bartender put his hands up. "Look, guys, I don't want any trouble here. Why don't you two just go back out the same way you came in?"

Vinnie's hand went for the Glock, but a door opened up behind the bar and Nicky Needles emerged. He looked up from some receipts and he saw the two men. He recognized Joe and stopped dead in his tracks. "Why are you here?"

"Why do you think I'm here?" Joe asked.

Nicky said nothing.

"You hear about Gonzo and Jonesy yet?"

"No," Nicky said. "What about 'em?"

Vinnie grinned. "They're waiting for you."

"Where?"

"In hell."

An expression of concern washed over Nicky's face. He went for his gun—a .38 police special tucked into his waistband—but Joe had the big Smith & Wesson trained on him before he could get to it. The bartender came up from behind the bar with a pump shotgun, but Vinnie shot him in the shoulder with the Glock before he could do any damage. The shotgun fell to the ground and the bartender moaned in agony.

"Pick up that shotgun and give it to me," Joe said.

The bartender sheepishly gave him the gun.

Vinnie held up the Glock, showed it to everyone sitting in the bar. "Anyone else wants to get involved, you'll get shot, too. I got plenty of bullets, so come on up." No one moved or said a word.

Joe stood there, shotgun slung over his shoulder, Smith & Wesson out, staring at Nicky. "You and I are gonna have a little talk."

Nicky grinned. "You're just sore cause I kicked your ass."

"I'll bet money you're not so tough when you don't have a pistol in someone's face," Joe said. "I don't think you'll be kicking my ass today."

"Where you wanna talk?"

"You're leaving with us," Joe said.

Vinnie yelled out to the bar's patronage again. "Nicky Needles is not worth losing your life over. Anyone says shit to the cops, I'll come back here myself and kill every one of you motherfuckers. Got it?"

As they were walking out, the jukebox started playing another David Allan Coe ditty about black people. Joe racked the shotgun once and shot the jukebox, effectively ending the music. Joe turned to the bartender, "Next time get better music."

A few minutes later the three men were in Vinnie's Lincoln Navigator. With Vinnie driving, Nicky rode in the passenger seat. Joe sat in the back, his shotgun aimed at Nicky's head.

"Why are you doing this?" Nicky asked.

"Two reasons," Joe said. "To find out about my daughter, and for good old-fashioned revenge."

"You gonna kill me?"

"What do you think?"

Nicky's eyes were as big as saucers. "What if I tell you what you want to know? Will you still kill me?"

"Now isn't the time for this," Joe said. "We can talk about this when we get where we're going."

"Please," Nicky said.

Joe pushed the barrel of the shotgun against the back of Nicky's head. "Just shut up and ride."

Within minutes Joe, Vinnie, and Nicky were walking along the pedestrian walkway of the Whitestone Bridge. Nicky walked out front, with Joe and Vinnie behind, their pistols still out. Cars and trucks passed by, their passengers no doubt seeing the guns, but everyone pretended to see nothing and went on their merry way.

"How far we gonna walk?" Nicky asked.

"Just keep walking," Joe said.

Vinnie added, "We'll let you know when we get there."

"You guys must be nuts," Nicky said. "You gonna kill me out here in the middle of the fucking Whitestone suspension bridge? You're out of your fucking minds."

"Shut up and keep walking asshole," Vinnie said.

"Let's talk about this," Nicky said. "Tell me what you want to know."

Irritated, Joe said, "What I want to know is whether or not you can walk to the middle of this bridge without talking."

Vinnie chuckled. Nicky took the hint and kept his mouth shut.

Finally when they were close to the middle of the bridge, Joe said, "Stop here."

Nicky looked down at the water. "How high you figure we are?"

"I'm gonna say about a hundred and fifty feet," Vinnie said.

"Nah," Joe said. "It's one hundred and thirty-eight feet."

"How you know that?" Nicky asked.

"I read, asshole. But I'm not here to discuss the fucking bridge."

Nicky nodded. "What do you wanna know?"

"Who hired you?"

"For what?"

"The job at my home."

"Ronnie Gates, the guy with all the acne scars on his face."

Joe looked out over the water. "The one that looks like a cop?"

"Yeah," Nicky said, nodding. "He used to be NYPD, but he went to jail for selling meth and stealing evidence. Now he's the Greek's go-to-guy. He does hits and oversees day-to-day operations for the Greek."

"Who the fuck is *the Greek*?" Joe asked.

"Nikos Panagakos," Nicky said.

"Small-time gangster and Mafia wannabe," Vinnie said. "Has operations in several cities around the U.S., but calls New York home."

Joe bit his lip. "So this job was ordered by this guy, the Greek?"

"I can't say for sure," Nicky said, "but I would imagine so. Ronnie called with the job and I didn't ask any questions. He just told me to round up some guys and I did. I figured a job's a job."

"Any idea how they picked my buddy Joe here for the job?" Vinnie asked.

"No idea. I thought it was kind of weird, since Joe was just a writer, but I figured they knew what they were doing. And I guess it worked. I saw on TV you killed the old greaseball in that hotel."

"My uncle Carlo," Vinnie said. "Carlo Ventimiglia."

Nicky looked around nervously. "Uh, sorry. I didn't know he was your uncle."

"I'll try to remember that," Vinnie said.

Joe spoke up. "What about my little girl?"

"What about her?"

"Where is she?"

"They didn't bring her back?"

"No."

"That's crazy. That doesn't make any sense."

"Right. So you don't know where she is?"

"No idea," Nicky said.

"Were you there when they took her from the bus stop?"

"Yeah. I was the one who put her in the trunk."

Joe raised the Smith & Wesson to Nicky's head. "Strike one, asshole."

"Sorry," Nicky said, sweat pouring down his face. "I didn't hurt her. I swear."

"Well, that's a plus."

"You know these kinds of people better than I do," Joe said. "Why would they kidnap a little girl?"

"If I was gonna do it, I'd do it for the ransom money," Nicky said. "But they didn't do that, so I'm not sure. I hear there are brothels down in Mexico who buy little girls. I've also heard tales of drug smugglers hollowing out the insides of little kids and using them as mules. They say they fill their insides with drugs."

Nicky realized who he was talking to and stopped talking. "Sorry," he said.

Joe started to lose it. He found himself on the verge of tears, the gun shaking in his hand.

"How do we find Ronnie Gates?" Vinnie asked.

"Ronnie's not hard to find," Nicky said. "His office is in the back of this little tattoo parlor in the Village."

"How many people are usually working in there?" Vinnie asked.

"One or two ink slingers, and Ronnie's bodyguard."

"Ronnie got a bodyguard?"

"Yeah, big Samoan sonofabitch."

"You know the address of this tattoo parlor?" Joe asked.

"No," Nicky said, "but it's in the book. Murder Ink Body Arts."

"Anything else you can tell us about that night at Joe's house?" Vinnie asked.

Nicky looked at Joe. "I swear I didn't know they were gonna kill your wife."

Joe looked up, his expression intense. "Really?"

"I swear, man."

"The way you kept kicking the shit out of me and laughing, I really doubt you would have had any trouble with them murdering Denise."

"Denise?" Nicky said. "Her name was Denise?"

"Yeah," Joe said, sticking the Smith & Wesson in Nicky's face. "And you don't get to say her name."

Vinnie moved toward Nicky, pushing him back against the railing. He pressed the barrel of his Glock against Nicky's left cheek. The barrel of Joe's Smith & Wesson already rested against Nicky's right cheek.

Tears started trickling down Nicky's cheeks. "There must be something I can do or say..."

"No," Joe said. "There's no way to talk your way out of this."

"Why?"

"You bastards didn't give Denise the opportunity to talk her way out of it."

Vinnie grinned slightly. "Any last words, scumbag?"

Nicky thought for a second and then said, "I'm sorry."

Joe nodded. "Duly noted."

Joe and Vinnie looked at each other and then back at Nicky. They pulled their triggers simultaneously. Nicky's body fell back and flipped over the railing of the bridge, and he fell into the East River.

Vinnie looked at Joe and said, "You hungry?"

Joe was tired as hell but said, "I could eat."

DAY EIGHT: PART ONE

Joe toiled in the garage, listening to a Billy Joel CD on repeat and modifying the shotgun he'd taken from the bartender at The Rabid Rabbit. It was only nine a.m. and he'd already removed the stock from the rifle and sanded it down smooth. Now he had the barrel of the shotgun clamped in a vise and used a panel saw to cut the barrel down to size. This would make the shotgun easier to conceal and would also remove the choke, giving the pellets a wider spread when fired.

Joe took a drink of his beer. Billy Joel was singing "Big Shot" when Vinnie stepped into the garage.

"I thought maybe you tried to make a run for it," Vinnie said.

"Nah. I just thought I'd modify this shotgun before we go after Ronnie Gates."

"And the Greek. Let's not forget him."

"You planning on going after them both today?"

"No time like the present."

"Sounds good to me."

"So, you like Billy Joel?"

"Yeah. You?"

"Not really. My old man was a big Billy Joel fan though. His favorite was 'Scenes from an Italian Restaurant.'"

Joe nodded. "Good song." He went back to sawing the shotgun barrel.

"I'm gonna go in and take a shower. I figure we'll go see old Ronnie boy in maybe thirty, forty minutes."

"Sounds like a plan."

"You got another beer in the fridge?"

"Help yourself."

"Thanks." Vinnie turned and walked back toward the house.

Joe and Vinnie pulled up in front of the tattoo parlor and parked the Navigator right there on the street. The shop's windows had a light tint on them, so Joe and Vinnie couldn't see how many people were inside. Joe and Vinnie both had their pistols out already, Joe with the sawed-off shotgun down beside his right leg.

Vinnie led the way. A bell jingled when he opened the door. There were two tattoo artists—a man and a woman—goofing around in the shop, but no one paid Vinnie any mind. The man tinkered with one of the tattooing chairs, his back to them, and the woman sat in the corner, reading a magazine. After they were both inside the store, Vinnie said, "Get the sign," and locked the front door. Joe went to the neon "OPEN" sign and unplugged it from the wall beneath the window.

Now the tattoo artists were looking at them. "What do you think you're doing?" asked the guy. Joe thought he looked like a retarded, tatted-up, Henry Rollins. He wore a sleeveless shirt to show off his muscles. He probably thought this would be intimidating as he moved towards Joe and Vinnie. When Joe racked the shotgun, however, Retarded Henry Rollins stood down. He put his hands up, palms out. "Whoa, hold it there, partner," he said.

Vinnie aimed the Glock at him. "You keep your mouth shut and do as you're told, you just might live through the day. Where's Ronnie?"

The guy played dumb. "Ronnie who?"

Joe pointed the shotgun at him, and suddenly the guy remembered. "Oh, *Ronnie*," he said. "Ronnie's in the back."

"Hey, you," Joe said to the girl, still reading her magazine.
"Yeah?"

"You got any tape?"

She looked at him like he was an idiot. "What kind of tape?"

"You know, the thick, silver kind."

"Duct tape?"

"Yeah, duct tape."

"Why the fuck would we have duct tape?"

"I need something to tie you up with, so we can keep you out of the way."

"I don't think it matters much," Retarded Henry Rollins said.

Vinnie looked at him. "What makes you say that?"

"I'm pretty sure they already know you're here."

"What makes you say that?"

Retarded Henry Rollins pointed to a surveillance camera mounted on the ceiling in the corner of the room.

"Good Christ," Vinnie said. He looked at the girl. "How many people are back there?"

The girl rolled her eyes, started to say something smart, but the door to Ronnie's office opened and the big Samoan came out firing a .45, a shot hitting the girl square in the temple. She fell to the floor in a bloody mess. Retarded Henry Rollins started towards her. "*Adrian!*" he shouted, as a bullet hit him in the side of the head, just beneath his ear.

Vinnie moved to the left side of the hallway where the Samoan shot from. Joe moved to the right, a bullet just missing his head as he did so. Vinnie peeked around the corner, seeing the Samoan in a mirror hanging in the hallway. He wore oversized hip-hop clothing and a big gold chain around his neck. The Samoan fired another shot from his .45, nearly hitting Vinnie's face.

For a moment there was silence. Vinnie said, "Stop shooting. We just want to talk." Another .45 shot rang out from the hallway, the round striking one of the swiveling tattoo chairs.

Joe looked at Vinnie. "Here goes nothing." Joe jumped into the mouth of the hallway, shotgun out, and fired the thing right at the Samoan. The blast from the shotgun struck the big sonofabitch in the chest and sent him flying back through the semi-closed door behind him. As he fell, the Samoan fired off one last shot into the wall beside him.

Joe moved quickly towards the door. As he did so, he switched the Smith & Wesson and the shotgun from one hand to the other. Now he had the Smith & Wesson up, ready to go through the door. Vinnie came right behind him.

"Come out, come out, wherever you are," Vinnie said.

A single shot came through the door in response.

"Seriously. Put the fucking gun down or we're gonna kill you."

It was dead silent for a moment before Ronnie spoke. "You're not gonna kill me?"

"Not if you tell us what we wanna know."

"How do I know you'll keep your word?"

Joe spoke up. "Ronnie, it's Joe Gibson. I'm not a criminal. I'm a normal guy. I don't like you at all. In fact, I fucking hate your guts. But I'm a man of my word. You put the gun down and talk to us, I promise I won't kill you."

"What about the other guy?"

Joe looked at Vinnie. "I promise you that neither of us will shoot you."

"You *promise*?"

"Scout's honor."

Vinnie became impatient. "You gonna put the gun down or what, asshole?"

"I'm putting it down," Ronnie said.

"It's down now?"

"It's down."

Joe started toward the door. "We're coming in. So help me God if you shoot at me—"

"You shoot at him," Vinnie said, "and I guarantee you that you're dead."

"No, no," Ronnie said. "The gun is down, the gun is down."

Joe stepped over the Samoan's body and found himself inside the ugliest office he'd ever seen. The walls had been painted red, and there were framed photographs of Ronnie with all types of celebrities, from Joe Montana to Christopher Lloyd. Ronnie knelt behind the big oak desk, his .45 sitting on top of it.

"You've met a lot of famous people," Joe said, looking at the photos.

Ronnie beamed. "I'm pretty proud of these."

Joe was looking at a photograph of Ronnie shaking hands with Bob Barker when Vinnie said, "You wanna meet any more celebrities—living ones, at least—you'll tell us what we need to know."

Ronnie nodded his head like a bobble-head doll. "Anything, guys, anything."

"Stand up," Vinnie said, "and sit in the chair so we can talk like normal human beings."

"Okay." Ronnie stood up and sat in the chair.

"Who was behind the job at Joe's house?" Vinnie asked.

Ronnie didn't hesitate. "It was the Greek. The Greek sent us there, told us to take the little girl, told us to tell Joe to kill Ventimiglia."

Joe's Smith & Wesson was trained on Ronnie. "The Greek tell you to kill my wife?"

Ronnie looked around nervously. "Yeah."

"Why?"

"He wanted you to know we meant business."

"Why'd he pick me for this little caper?"

Ronnie shook his head. "I really don't know. I've been curious about that. I asked him once, but he said, 'Don't worry about it,' told me to mind my own fucking business. But yeah, I thought it was weird."

"I never hurt anybody in my entire life..."

"You sure hurt the fuck out of old man Ventimiglia," Ronnie said.

Joe and Vinnie exchanged a knowing glance.

"And Denise, she sure as hell never hurt anybody."

Joe straightened his arm, repositioning the gun in Ronnie's face.

Ronnie put his hands up. "I thought you said you wouldn't kill me."

"You tell him what he wants to know, he ain't gonna kill you," Vinnie said.

"Why'd the Greek want my daughter?" Joe asked.

"She was supposed to be insurance—to make you do what the Greek wanted you to do."

"So why didn't he give her back?"

"He didn't expect you to succeed, and he really didn't expect you to survive. He sold the little girl to some backwoods bayou brothel before you even went to that hotel."

"Where is she now?" Joe asked, the tears starting to come.

"I don't know. I'm sure she's in Louisiana by now, turning tricks or whatever."

"Do you want to live?" Joe asked.

Ronnie said he did.

"Then you pick up that telephone."

"Who am I calling?"

"The Greek. And so help me, if you tip him off in any way, I'll blow your fucking head off."

Ronnie picked up the phone. "What do I tell him?"

"Tell him you're coming to see him."

"Today?"

"Now. And you better put on a swell performance. I mean, it better be a dandy, because if I get so much as an inkling of an idea that you're selling us out, your brains are gonna be all over these walls."

Ronnie dialed the phone. He listened for a moment and then said, "Yeah, this is Ronnie. Lemme talk to the boss." Ronnie listened silently for about thirty seconds before saying, "Yeah, Boss. I gotta talk to you about some things, but I don't wanna do it over the phone. If you don't mind, I'm coming over." Another pause and then Ronnie said, "I'm on my way."

Ronnie hung up the telephone. "Now what?"

Vinnie said, "Now we go meet the man."

Mertis Whitlock stopped by Joe Gibson's place just after eleven. Gibson's Ford Expedition sat in the driveway, so Mertis figured he was home. Mertis climbed out of the Crown Vic, lit a cigarette, and made his way up towards the porch. He knocked on the door several times but no one answered. He walked down around the porch. He could hear music—sounded like Billy Joel—coming from the garage, some ten feet further up the driveway beyond the Expedition.

As Mertis made his way around the house, he saw the garage door standing open. He envisioned Gibson back there tinkering around at his workbench.

"Mr. Gibson?" Mertis said.

No answer.

Billy Joel sang "We Didn't Start the Fire," a song that Mertis didn't particularly care for. Mertis noticed the can of beer sitting there on the workbench. He touched it to see if it was still cold, but found it to be warm. Mertis was about to call out for Gibson again when he noticed the sawed-off shotgun barrel clamped in the vise.

"Shit," Mertis said.

At once he knew Gibson was out for revenge against the bastards who'd taken his little girl. Mertis couldn't fault him for going after the kidnappers, but he also knew that the law was the law. At least for now, until after he'd spoken to Gibson about all of this, Mertis decided not to say anything to anyone about what he'd discovered.

DAY EIGHT: PART TWO

The three men took Ronnie's Cutlass Supreme to see the Greek. When Vinnie started the car, Conway Twitty's "Hello Darling" came blaring from the speakers. Vinnie quickly rectified this by ejecting the CD and tossing it out the window. At first Ronnie objected, but Vinnie reminded him that he was lucky to even be alive.

"You sure the Greek's gonna be home?" Vinnie asked.

Ronnie nodded. "He does all his business there. He never leaves."

"How many men does he have with him?"

"He keeps a small army in there."

"How many men?"

"I'm not sure."

"Guess."

Ronnie rubbed his chin, thinking. "I'd say twenty, maybe more."

Vinnie laughed.

"How can you laugh?" Joe asked from the backseat. "We could get killed in there."

"A guy's gotta die some time, Joe. Besides, what do you care? Your time is coming pretty soon either way."

Ronnie thought about this for a moment. He started to comment, but Joe pressed the Smith & Wesson against the back of his head. "Mind your own business."

Nikos Panagakos, also known as the Greek, lived in a swanky neighborhood on the Upper East Side. He had a mansion that looked like the kind of place a hip-hop music mogul would own. At once both stately and gaudy, the Greek's home had the Spanish structural design that was much more prevalent in California. There it would likely have been surrounded by palm trees. Here it was only surrounded by the Greek's goons, standing guard. There were two of them out in front of the place, on opposite sides of the yard. Their guns weren't out, but they were obviously packing.

Vinnie pulled the Cutlass into the driveway, parking behind four black Cadillacs.

"Let's run through this," Vinnie said. "We're gonna have our guns holstered, Ronnie. But so help me God, you pull any shit, you die. Simple as that."

Ronnie chuckled. "You must be pretty quick on the draw."

"I'm Wyatt fucking Earp," Vinnie said, chewing on a toothpick. "Don't try me."

"You guys promise you're not gonna kill me?"

"We won't kill you," Joe said. "All you gotta do is go through the motions, act like it's business as usual, and get us inside that house."

"That shouldn't be a problem."

The three men got out of the car. Ronnie led the way up the driveway, with Vinnie and Joe right behind. One of the goons patrolling the yard called out to Ronnie, "Hey chief, how's it going?"

Ronnie played it cool. "Not bad. And yourself?"

"Another day, another dollar."

Ronnie smirked and nodded, walking up the steps to the front door.

"You guys ready for this?" he asked.

"Ready as I'll ever be," Joe said.

Ronnie knocked. A man opened the door just a crack, peering out through the chain-lock.

"It's me," Ronnie said. "The boss is expecting us."

"Gimme a minute."

The man called someone on a walkie-talkie. "Ronnie's here. Got two guys with him." He waited for a few seconds and then a voice said, "Send 'em on back." The man said "Okay," and unlocked the door. When he did, Vinnie turned and fired on the goon who'd said "another day, another dollar" to Ronnie. The bullet struck the man center mass in the back, and he dropped. Vinnie whirled around and fired on the second goon, shooting him in the face.

Joe followed right behind Ronnie. He reached over Ronnie's shoulder and fired into the doorman's face. Joe then grabbed Ronnie from behind and shoved him into the doorway, firing upon the Greek's men from around his body. First he shot a man to the left, and then he shot a goon just to the right. Ronnie started to blurt something out about not being able to hear anything due to Joe's gunshots next to his ear, but a hail of bullets struck him from the front. As Ronnie fell dead to the ground, both Joe and Vinnie came up firing from behind.

Vinnie shot a big Latino with a .45 standing on the stairway in the chest. The man lost his balance and toppled down the stairs, landing in a bloody heap. A large Italian man in a bright blue and orange Hawaiian shirt sat at a table to their left. Joe fired on the man before he could reach for his weapon. The bullet struck him in the nose, and the man's face slammed forward into the bowl of Fruity Pebbles he'd been eating.

A heavyset black man with a Beretta emerged from a hallway at the back of the room. "What the fuck goin' on out here?" Vinnie shot him in the chest. The man staggered for a second, looked around with an expression of confusion, and finally fell, taking a small decorative table down with him.

No one else was visible in the two front rooms. Joe and Vinnie moved quickly, making their way toward the bowels of the estate. An attractive woman, probably twenty-five or so, emerged on the stairway just above the dead Latino. Joe raised the Smith & Wesson, but decided to let her go since she wasn't one of the Greek's soldiers. As he lowered the pistol, the woman pulled out a snub-nosed .38 and aimed it at Joe. Vinnie fired on her before she could shoot, hitting her in the forehead, and she flopped down the stairs.

Joe looked at Vinnie. "Thanks."

"Don't mention it," Vinnie said. "We'd better reload while we can. Me first, then you."

The two men took turns reloading their weapons. They then moved quietly into the hallway from which the black man had emerged. Joe led the way, with Vinnie watching their rear. Joe came to a couple of rooms, pushing their doors open, and finding no one inside. Joe saw a closed door at the end of the hall. He crept toward it. He saw a movement in the light beneath the door, realized what was happening, and said, "Oh Jesus." He managed to dive out of the way just in time, as a shotgun blast splintered the door to pieces.

The guy inside, another Latino, made the mistake of peering out through the hole in the door. When he did, Vinnie shot him square in the face, and the man went down.

"You all right?" Vinnie asked.

Joe raised himself up from the floor. "Yeah."

Joe led the way again, and the two men entered the room at the end of the hallway. There was no one inside other than the dead Latino with the scatter gun. The room looked like a sort of break room for the Greek's men—bare with only two picnic tables in the center of the room. A refrigerator and a microwave were the room's only adornments. A small television sat in the corner, an old black-and-white western on the screen, a shoot-out taking place between a gang of outlaws and a pursuing posse.

When Joe opened the door on the other side of the break room, he found himself in another hallway. A door ahead and to the left opened and a heavyset man with a pistol emerged. The man spotted Joe and raised his gun, but Joe shot him in the throat.

"Nice shootin', Tex," Vinnie said.

Before the words were out of Vinnie's mouth, a Puerto Rican popped up behind him. Joe saw the guy, but couldn't move fast enough to stop him from shooting Vinnie in the left shoulder. So the Puerto Rican popped off his shot, and then Joe shot him in the cheek, blowing his brains out.

"You all right?" Joe asked.

"Fuck no," Vinnie said. "It hurts like a sonofabitch."

"You'll live?"

"Yeah, I'll live. But I could sure use a smoke right about now."

Joe turned and pushed the next door open, finding no one inside. He then moved on to the next door, on his right, and looked inside. A bathroom, no one inside. The next door he came to was the one from which the heavyset man had emerged. It was a bedroom, and it was empty.

Joe stepped over the body and moved toward the closed door at the end of the hallway. He carefully opened it and found a large rec room. It had a bar on one end, a pool table and an air hockey table in the center, and a variety of vintage arcade games lining the walls. At the far end of the room, near the bar, a young black guy listened to loud music in headphones and played Ms. Pac-Man, completely oblivious to all the ruckus. The guy completed another level on the game when Joe stepped up behind him, pushing the barrel of the Smith & Wesson against the back of his head.

The guy jumped, startled. "Fuck you doin'?" he asked, his eyes big and crazy. The gun in his face now, he pulled off the headphones. "Who the fuck are you supposed to be?"

Joe nodded towards the game. "You're pretty good."

"Yeah, well, I play a lot."

"That what you do for the Greek, play video games?"

The guy shrugged. "It passes the time."

Vinnie said, "Here's one for you, Einstein. Imagine you were in here playing your stupid fucking game and listening to your music, and the house was overrun. I bet you wouldn't even know." He looked at Joe. "What do you think?"

"Nah," Joe said. "I doubt you'd have even the slightest clue."

The guy looked shocked. "You guys overran the house?"

Vinnie nodded.

"How many people are dead out there?"

"All of 'em," Joe said.

"Everyone we saw, anyway," Vinnie added.

"Damn," the guy said. "So now you gonna kill me?"

"Depends," Joe said.

"On what?"

"On how much you cooperate."

"You say *everyone's* dead?"

Vinnie nodded again.

"Shit, I don't wanna die. You ain't gotta ask me twice. What you wanna know?"

Joe and Vinnie looked at each other, grinning.

Joe said, "We can't find the Greek."

"You didn't see him while you were playin' *Wild Bunch* out there?"

"Un-uh."

"Shit, he's probably locked away down in the safe room."

"Can you get in?" Vinnie asked.

"The safe room?"

"Yeah."

"Sure. That all you need?"

Vinnie laughed. "You'd give up your boss' life to save your black ass?"

"Nigga, I'd give up my *mama's* life to save my black ass."

The guy, who identified himself as Tyrone, led them through a series of hallways and stairs. On the way, Tyrone said, "Can I ask you a question?"

"Anything," Vinnie said.

"While you guys were shootin' up the place, you happen to notice a fat bastard in an ugly-ass Hawaiian shirt?"

"Yeah," Joe said. "The guy with the cereal."

"You guys kill him?"

"Yeah. Why?"

"That nigga Chuck still owes me twenty dollars."

Joe ignored this. "What's the safe room like?"

"It's just an empty room with nothing in it but a bed, a table, and a refrigerator. It's got concrete and steel-reinforced walls. The Greek says you'd have to have a bazooka to get inside."

"We won't need a bazooka," Vinnie said.

"Nah," Joe said, looking at Tyrone. "We got you."

"My lucky day," Tyrone said.

Finally Tyrone brought them to a closed steel door with an intercom system next to it, two levels beneath the ground.

"This is the safe room?" Joe asked.

Tyrone nodded. "This is it."

Vinnie pointed his .45 at Tyrone. "Do your thing, buddy."

"Put that motherfuckin' gun down and I will. I don't do shit with a gun in my face."

Vinnie gave Joe a "fuck this guy" look and lowered the pistol. "Go to it."

Tyrone pushed the button on the intercom.

"Who is it?" asked a husky voice.

"It's Tyrone. Let me in the goddamn door, Jake."

"What's the password?"

Tyrone looked at Joe and Vinnie, shaking his head. "Kumbaya, my Lord."

There was a moment of silence and then the door opened. Jake, a big burly guy, stood there looking stupid just before Vinnie shot him in the chest.

This left only the Greek, a heavyset, old man with liver spots who reminded Joe of Anthony Quinn. The Greek looked at Tyrone. "What the hell did you let them in here for?"

"What?" Tyrone asked. "And get *my* ass killed? Hell no."

Tyrone started to talk some more shit when Vinnie raised the .45, pointing it at the back of his head. "Sorry, Tyrone," Vinnie said, pulling the trigger.

Noticeably perturbed, the Greek said, "Fuck you do that for?"

"To get your attention," Vinnie said.

"Trust me, you got my attention when you wiped out all my men."

Joe stuck the Smith & Wesson in the old man's face.

"Watch where you put that thing," the Greek said. "I'd hate to have to stick it up your ass."

"Big talk for an old man sitting in front of a .45 and a great big Smith & Wesson," Vinnie said, looking at Joe. "What do they call that thing?"

"The Governor," Joe said.

"I've got to say, I never imagined you getting this far," the Greek said. "The way you took out Ventimiglia and all his guys—"

"And all *your* guys," Joe said.

"Right," the Greek said, grinning. "Very impressive. In another life, who knows? You coulda been one of us."

"Why the fuck did you pick *me* to go after Ventimiglia?" Joe asked. "I've never understood that."

"Yeah," Vinnie said, nodding. "That shit don't make sense."

The Greek smiled. "You sure you want to hear this?"

Joe looked at Vinnie, then back at the Greek. "Let's hear it."

"Well, we were having problems with Ventimiglia. We were trying to expand to Chicago, but he kept fucking with us. So, I decided, the old bastard had to go. I didn't want me or any of my guys connected to the hit. Who needs that kind of shit storm raining down on their head? So, I decided to have a regular guy—a, uh, *regular Joe*, if you will—" The Greek laughed at his own joke. "I decided to have him kill Ventimiglia for me. I figured it would be easy—all I'd have to do is threaten to take away their loved ones and they'd do it. I got the idea from that movie—"

"The one with Johnny Depp?" Vinnie asked.

"No. It was an older movie with, uh, Ben Gazzara in it. You seen it?"

Vinnie shook his head. "No, I don't think so."

Joe didn't care about any of this. "So why *me*? How the fuck did you select *me* for this little adventure?"

"You'll love this," the Greek said.

"Somehow I kinda doubt that."

"I was reading one of your books. It was *No Rest for the Wicked*. Pretty good book. At least the first half. I didn't care much for the conclusion. Seemed kind of contrived."

Joe pressed the barrel of the Smith & Wesson against the Greek's nose. "Go on."

"Anyway, I was trying to figure out how I would go about selecting someone for the job. Then, I look down at the book, and lo and behold, there's your picture on the back. And your bio said you lived in New York City with your wife and daughter, and I thought, 'Well, shit, it's my lucky day.'"

Joe couldn't believe what he was hearing. "*That's* how you selected me?"

The Greek smiled big, obviously quite proud of himself.

Joe swung the Smith & Wesson hard across the Greek's face, pistol-whipping the old man. The Greek's head rocked sideways and a mixture of blood and teeth flew from his mouth. He shook his head, trying to clear his vision, blood dripping from his lips.

"Nice swing, kid," he said.

Joe wasn't laughing. "Why'd you kill Denise?"

The Greek looked confused. "Who the fuck is Denise?"

"My wife, asshole!" Joe swung the Smith & Wesson again—harder this time—and managed to knock out a few more of the Greek's teeth.

"Sorry," the Greek said, still grinning. "Your wife... Well, I just wanted you to know we meant business."

"You took my daughter," Joe said. "I think I would have known you meant business without your killing my wife."

"We had to be sure we had you by the *cojones*. We had to know you wouldn't go to the cops."

"Well, I didn't. And I did what you wanted. So why didn't you bring back my daughter?"

"Who knew you'd make it out of there alive? The odds were a million to one. So I figured, hey, I'd make some money off the little girl. Sold her to a couple of brothel owners down in Louisiana, go by the name of the Kleek brothers."

There were tears in Joe's eyes again. "Where is she now?"

"Like I said, I sold her to the Kleek brothers. I suspect she's down there in Louisiana, working in that brothel."

Joe started shaking. Badly. He repositioned the pistol, pressing it right between the Greek's eyes.

"Before I kill you," Joe said, "I have to know one thing."

"Which is?"

"How much money did you get for my little Emily?"

The Greek smiled, his mouth a bloody mess. "Ten thousand."

"You sold my eight-year-old daughter for ten thousand dollars?"

"Yeah."

Joe pulled the trigger, and the Greek was no more.

DAY EIGHT: PART THREE

Dewayne and Arturo had been watching the little girl for a week now, and the shit had gotten old fast. Someone was supposed to have come to pick her up two days ago, but there had been a delay. Dewayne was starting to miss the outside world. He'd been cooped up in the little house for the past seven days, with no one to keep him company but Arturo and the old black-and-white television. This sucked, as Arturo didn't talk much and the television only picked up two channels.

Dewayne had started watching the little girl—really paying attention to her—about three days ago. He couldn't say exactly when he'd developed the taste for little girls—maybe during his stretch in Lompoc—but it was certainly there now. Try as he might, he couldn't get the thoughts of that little girl and all the things he could do to her out of his head. So far it hadn't been a problem, as he hadn't had more than two minutes alone with her. But today would be different. Today Arturo announced that he was going out for food.

"I'm sick of eating ramen noodles every meal," Arturo said.

"What's wrong with ramen noodles?" Dewayne had asked.

"Fuck ramen noodles. I've eaten so many ramen noodles this week that I've got 'em coming out my ass. If I never eat another ramen noodle again, it'll be too soon."

And Arturo left.

Emily was scared and she missed her parents. She didn't know what exactly was happening to her, but she knew it was wrong. The two guys—the one with the brown skin and the one with the white skin—were nice enough to her, but she sensed that this wasn't supposed to be happening. "We're gonna watch you until your Mommy and Daddy come home," the brown-skinned one had told her.

"Where did they go?" she asked.

"Mommy and Daddy had to go on a trip. It was real urgent and they didn't have time to tell you goodbye. But they asked us to watch you until they get back."

The brown-skinned man was okay, but the other one—the one who told her to call him Uncle Dewayne—was much nicer. Emily couldn't put her finger on it, but she sensed there was something wrong with him. The way he looked at her. Something was weird about it.

Emily sat on the bean bag in the room they had given her, watching *The Flintstones* on an old VHS tape. She had already seen this episode many times over the past week, but watching it beat doing nothing.

The door opened, and the one who called himself Uncle Dewayne entered. And Emily knew at once there was something different about him.

"You and I are gonna play," he said.

Emily looked at him. "Can we play with the toys?"

"What toys?"

"The ones in the closet."

"There are toys in the closet?"

Emily pointed at the closet. "Way up at the top, on one of the shelves. You can see Monopoly and some other games up there, and there are toys stacked on top of the boxes—a teddy bear and some other stuff."

Dewayne rubbed his chin. "I wonder why those are up there."

Dewayne walked to the closet and looked inside. Looking up, he said, "Sure, I'll get 'em down. One of those games is Twister. Have you ever played Twister?"

Emily said she had not.

"Well," Dewayne said, "you and I can play us a game of Twister. I think you'll like it."

He winked at her.

He then stood up and walked out of the room. He left for about thirty seconds, and then returned with a wooden crate.

"I'll just climb up on this and get those toys down. Then we can play Twister."

Dewayne climbed on top of the crate, but still had difficulty reaching the toys. He stood on his tip-toes, and managed to pull down the stack of games and toys. Just when he retrieved the toys, however, the crate caved in and Dewayne came crashing down to the floor, hitting his head in the process.

Emily picked up an Etch-a-Sketch that had fallen with Dewayne, and looked at it for a moment. Dewayne blinked and tried to focus his eyes, but Emily smashed the Etch-a-Sketch over his face as hard as she could. Dewayne made a moaning sound when the toy struck his face, and he was out cold.

Emily turned and ran through the open door, and then ran out of the house.

Mertis Whitlock sat at his desk, looking over crime scene photographs of the Hyperion Hotel massacre when Johnson, a uniformed cop, approached his desk. Mertis didn't look up.

"Detective Whitlock?" Johnson asked.

"Yeah, what is it?"

"I've got something you're gonna wanna see."

Mertis looked up and saw the teary-eyed little girl standing beside Johnson.

"I don't understand," Mertis said.

"We found her wandering around in an alley, crying and lost. They said we should bring her to you."

"Why is that?"

"Her name is Emily Gibson."

DAY EIGHT: PART FOUR

Vinnie and Joe were back in Vinnie's Navigator listening to some obnoxious song by Public Enemy that Joe neither liked nor understood. They were two blocks from Joe's house when Vinnie said, "I like you, Joe, but I'm still gonna have to kill you. Business is business."

Joe's grip tightened on the Smith & Wesson. "I'm afraid that's not gonna happen."

Vinnie looked at Joe, a smirk on his face. "Oh yeah? You don't think so?"

"Look," Joe said, "I just found out my little girl is alive and working in some goddamn brothel down in Louisiana. I'm gonna have to go find her. If you wanna kill me after that, then so be it. But I have to go get Emily."

"I get what you're saying, but I don't have that kind of time to wait."

Joe pulled the pistol up from beside his legs, sitting it on his lap. He gripped it tightly, making no effort to conceal the fact. "So how do you want to do this?"

"I really wanna let you go, honest I do. But if I go back to Chicago without your head on a platter, I'll be the one gets killed. And I can't have that, Joe. So I'm thinking—in about a minute we're gonna be right in front of your house. Suppose I let you run in the house and wait ten seconds to come in after you. Then, I kill you, you kill me, whatever..."

Joe looked at Vinnie and realized he'd come to like him. "I don't want to kill you."

"But I'll kill you. I'll kill the fuck out of you, Joe. I like you, but it ain't shit to me. So you gotta look at this as self-

74

preservation. It's kill or be killed, eat or fucking be eaten. Which one are you, Joe: are you Jaws or are you some dumb motherfucker on the beach that gets eaten by Jaws?"

Joe really didn't want to do this, but he played along. "I guess I'm Jaws."

"That's what I wanna hear."

Vinnie parked the Navigator in front of Joe's house.

He grinned and put out his hand for Joe to shake, and Joe shook it.

"You'd better get out now," Vinnie said. "Because I'm gonna start couting. Ten...nine..."

Joe opened the door, got out, and ran like a motherfucker.

Joe was crouched behind the couch when Vinnie got to the front door. Vinnie was angry and yelling about the door being locked. "Fuck you lock this door for, Joe? You really think that's gonna slow me down?"

Joe braced himself, arm over the couch, pistol trained on the front door.

Vinnie kicked the door open and started to step inside. The shot from Joe's Smith & Wesson just missed his head, and Vinnie ducked back out the door.

"Jesus Christ, Joe, you coulda killed me," Vinnie said, laughing at his own joke. "You wouldn't want to kill me, would you? I'm your buddy."

Vinnie stayed out of sight, and Joe kept the pistol trained on the doorway.

"What if you just stayed there with your gun aimed at the door," Vinnie said, "and I ran around the house and came in behind you through the back door? That would be something, huh?" Vinnie sounded irritated that Joe wasn't responding. "What's wrong, Joe? Cat got your tongue?"

Joe said nothing.

Vinnie took the hint and stopped talking. There was a long moment of silence—Joe thought it maybe two, three minutes—before Vinnie came diving through the door. It took Joe a millisecond to realize what was happening, and he fired late, missing Vinnie by a foot or so. Vinnie hit the ground and sort of rolled behind the wall to the stairs, where Joe couldn't see him.

"You like that?" Vinnie asked. "That looked like something out of a John Woo movie, didn't it? I took tumbling for two years as a kid. Always knew that would come in handy someday."

Joe fired into the wall, hoping to hit Vinnie.

Vinnie screeched. *"Oh shit, I'm hit!"*

Joe waited a few seconds before speaking. "You're hit?"

"Yeah, you hit me in the chest."

Joe didn't know what to say. "Is it bad?"

Vinnie sounded irritated. *"I'm hit in the fucking chest. Yes, goddammit, it's bad! How the hell could it possibly be good?"*

"Call this whole thing off, and I'll drive you to the hospital."

Joe could hear Vinnie sobbing. "I don't wanna die, Joe."

"Come on. We don't have to do this. You could just put down your gun and we could get you some help."

"I dunno."

"What's to know? If you don't get help, you're a dead man."

"Yeah," Vinnie said, "but if I let you go, I'm gonna die anyway."

"Maybe we can work that out together. Just put your gun down."

"And you'll put yours down, too?"

"Yeah. You put your gun down, I'll put my gun down."

"Okay, my gun is on the floor. Is yours?"

"Yes," Joe lied. "My gun is on the floor."

"Now what?"

"Now we take you to the hospital and get you patched—"

Vinnie came walking out from behind the corner, his pistol out. He fired once, his shot hitting the couch and just missing Joe by about an inch.

Joe still had his pistol trained on the corner where Vinnie was. He returned fire immediately, his shot striking Vinnie in the same shoulder he'd already been hit in at the Greek's place. Vinnie cried out in pain and spun around, falling out of sight.

"What the fuck?" Vinnie said. *"You lied!"*

"Well, you lied, too! You said your gun was down. And you said you were hit."

"You said *your* gun was down, goddammit!"

"I kind of figured you were gonna pull that shit," Joe said.

"You knew I was faking?"

"It seemed like something you would do. Hell, I would have done it."

Joe could hear Vinnie laughing. "I taught you well, my friend."

"Now what?"

"I guess now we get into some gangster shit, and we have us a good old-fashioned shoot-out."

"I was afraid you'd say that."

Joe turned and sprinted, heading for the kitchen.

Vinnie fired, his shot hitting the China cabinet ahead of Joe, just before Joe rounded the corner. Joe ran through the dining room and into the kitchen, ducking behind the cabinet island in the center of the room.

Vinnie was now in the dining room, hiding around the corner.

"Come on out, Joe," he said. "Why not make this easy for everybody?"

"Now what fun would that be?"

Vinnie fired into the kitchen, his shot hitting a frying pan hanging above Joe's head. The shot caromed off the pan and zipped into the wall.

"If you were me, what would *you* do?" Joe asked.

"Thank God I'm not you. But if I were you, I'd fight back. I'd fight back real hard, and I'd hope like hell that I won this little gunfight so I could go and save my little girl, Joe. That's what I would do."

Joe couldn't help himself—he actually liked this sonofabitch trying to kill him. "Yeah, that's pretty much where I'm at."

"Only problem with that," Vinnie said, "is that you can't beat me, Joe."

"Why is that?"

"I told you—I'm Wyatt fucking Earp."

Vinnie and Joe both laughed at this.

"You got your cigarettes on you, Joe?"

Joe wondered where this was going. "Yeah, why?"

"There's a real good chance at least one of us is gonna die, right?"

"Yeah."

"So what say you and I take a break and we each smoke a cigarette? Then, just as soon as we're both done with our cigarettes, we'll get back to killing one another."

This sounded like bullshit. "You fuckin' with me again, Vinnie?"

"No, I'm dead serious. I swear on a stack of Bibles. I swear on the Virgin Mary herself."

"You're Catholic?"

"I'm Italian, Joe. We're all Catholic."

"And you wanna take a break and smoke a cigarette?"

"I just wanna take a time out."

"A time out, huh?"

"Yeah, why not? I mean, I know it sounds silly, but it's just you and me here. Who's gonna know? Especially if we end up doing what we came here to do when we're finished with our cigarettes."

"You're serious?"

"As a heart-attack."

"Something is seriously wrong with you, my friend," Joe said. "And it's no small thing."

Vinnie laughed. "So we gonna do this, or what?"

Joe shrugged. "What the hell? A cigarette sounds pretty good right now."

Vinnie pulled the pack of Winstons from his jacket pocket, put one to his lips, and lit it. "I really do like you, Joe. I figure, if I gotta kill you, maybe we can just kind of sit here and shoot the shit for a few minutes first."

Joe lit his Pall Mall. "Shoot the shit, huh?"

"Yeah."

"What do you wanna talk about?"

"Why don't you tell me about Denise?"

Joe took a drag from the cigarette and exhaled. "Where do I begin? Denise was my life. I would have done anything for her."

"It shows."

"How so?"

"Look at all the people you've killed."

Joe smiled. "If you'd have told me two weeks ago that I would have killed all those people, I would have said you were crazy."

"Grief makes a person do strange things."

"I guess," Joe said. "How about you? You got a woman back home?"

Vinnie laughed. "I got lots of women back home."

"But no one special?"

"What are you talking about, Joe? They're *all* special. They're special for a night, and then they get dressed and they go home in the morning."

Joe laughed at this, and took another drag from his cigarette. "Don't you ever get lonely?"

"Nah, not really. I'm the kind of person who really likes being alone. I like being able to do what I want, when I want."

Joe nodded. "How'd you get into this line of work?"

Vinnie chuckled. "'*Line of work*,' huh?"

"Yeah."

"You know, it was the family business. My uncle was the fucking boss of Chicago. I never really had a choice." Vinnie took a drag of his cigarette. "How about you—how'd you end up becoming a writer?"

"It's all I ever wanted to be. For as long as I can remember I always wanted to write. When I was a kid I used to write stories about the characters in the books I read."

"What kinds of books?"

"*Treasure Island*, *Superman* comic books, shit like that. The usual."

"It wasn't usual for me," Vinnie said. "I hated to read when I was a kid. Only thing I ever read was a racing form."

"That's too bad. Did you ever want to be anything else besides a gangster?"

Vinnie thought about it for a minute. "Well, I really wanted to play shortstop for the Cubs. I wanted to be like Shawon Dunston. I had his poster hanging over my bed and everything."

"So what happened?"

Vinnie chuckled. "I couldn't hit the breaking pitch, that's what happened."

Joe laughed.

Vinnie stubbed out his cigarette against the wall. "I'm finished with my cigarette."

"Me too."

"You ready to do this?"

"Not really."

Each of them counted to ten in their heads before moving. And then they both emerged, pistols blazing. Vinnie's shot struck

Joe in the chest. Joe felt a burning near his heart. He gasped for air, but found it difficult to breathe. He staggered backwards in shock.

Shit, he'd really been hit.

Vinnie stood there for a moment, also in shock. Joe looked down at the bleeding wound, and then looked back up at Vinnie. Joe raised the Smith & Wesson and fired again, this time hitting Vinnie in the chest. The shot knocked Vinnie off his feet, and he was out cold.

Joe slid down against the cabinet. Breathing had become difficult, and Joe knew he was going to die. His shaking hands pulled out the pack of Pall Malls again, and he put one to his lips. He fumbled with his lighter for a moment before managing to light the damned thing.

He thought about his little Emily, and he closed his eyes.

CONCLUSION

Mertis hadn't gotten much out of Emily. She couldn't tell him exactly where she'd been kept, or who her keepers were. She'd given him the name "Dewayne," but had nothing more to offer. Mertis had then attempted to call Joe Gibson, but the phone went straight to voice mail. Probably out killing bad guys, Mertis thought. Hopefully he was wrong about Gibson. After all, little Emily was going to need her father.

They were driving in the Crown Vic, with Emily sitting in the backseat. She didn't speak at all on the drive over. Mertis tried to talk to her, but the little girl was having none of it. She just sat there in silence.

Mertis parked in the driveway behind Gibson's Expedition. There was also a black Navigator parked at the curb. Mertis sensed that something was wrong. He looked up and saw that the front door to the house was hanging open.

Then he heard gunshots.

He grabbed the CB and called for backup. Then he heard another shot.

He turned to the little girl. "Emily, you stay here. I'll be right back. Whatever you do, don't get out of this car until I get back here."

Mertis pulled out his .38 and ran onto the porch. He moved carefully into the house.

"Mr. Gibson?" he yelled out. There was no answer.

Mertis made his way through the house. He saw the broken China on the floor. He moved around the corner and saw what looked to be a dead man lying on the floor, a pistol next to him.

He moved towards the body, but then heard a moan coming from the kitchen.

"Gibson?" he called out.

"Yes?" the voice answered weakly.

Mertis moved carefully into the kitchen and around the cabinet island. There was Joe Gibson, leaning against the cabinet. He was a bloody mess. He was barely alive and smoking a cigarette. There was a big Smith & Wesson lying on the floor beside him.

Joe Gibson looked at him through squinted eyes.

"Hello, detective."

Mertis started to say something, but Vinnie's shot caught him in the throat. Mertis reached for the wound. Vinnie's second shot caught him in the chest, and Mertis fell to the floor.

"You didn't have to do that," Joe managed. "He was a really nice guy."

"He was a cop."

Vinnie dragged himself across the dining room and into the kitchen, leaving a trail of blood in his wake. He finally made it around the cabinet island.

"You gonna kill me now?" Joe asked.

"No offense, but I think I already did. And you definitely killed me. You and me, we're gonna sit here and die together."

Vinnie pulled himself up against the cabinet, and sat next to Joe.

"I should have worn a bulletproof vest," Vinnie said.

Joe forced himself to smile. "Me too."

Emily was tired of waiting. She had already waited a week to see her Mommy and Daddy, and she was ready to go into her house. She opened the car door and climbed out. She made her way up the steps and onto the porch. She looked at the broken door, but didn't understand what she was seeing. She went into the house and looked around for her parents. She saw the bullet hole in the wall beside the stairs, but didn't know what had caused it. She made her way into the dining room and saw the broken China all over the floor.

"Mommy?" she said. "Daddy?"

She looked down at the trail of blood which reached across the dining room carpet and onto the kitchen linoleum. She followed the it.

When she came around the cabinet island, she saw her daddy lying there hurt.

"Daddy," she yelled. *"Daddy, wake up!"*

Joe opened his eyes. It was blurry, but he saw his Emily standing there.

"Daddy?" she said, crying.

The voice sounded like it was far away.

Joe couldn't see much, but he could feel her nestling up against his bloody chest.

"Daddy, please," she sobbed.

And the voice was even farther away this time.

This, Joe thought, must be heaven, where people reunited with their loved ones. Here he would be with his little Emily again.

Would Denise be here, too?

"Please, Daddy, please."

The voice was so far away now.

Joe smiled and closed his eyes.

ABOUT THE AUTHOR

Andy Rausch is a freelance journalist, celebrity interviewer, and film critic. He is the author or co-author of nearly twenty books on the subject of popular culture. These include *Making Movies with Orson Welles*, *The Films of Martin Scorsese and Robert De Niro*, and *The Wit and Wisdom of Stephen King*. He is also the author of the novels *Elvis Presley, CIA Assassin, Mad World* and *Bloodletting*. He has also worked as an actor, film producer, composer, casting director, and as the screenwriter of the cult film *Dahmer vs. Gacy*. He is a regular contributor to *Screem* magazine, and his work has appeared in such publications and online journals as *Film Threat*, *Shock Cinema*, and *Bright Lights Film Journal*. He resides in Parsons, Kansas.

MAD WORLD BY ANDY RAUSCH

"*Mad World* is dark, twisted, no-holds-barred fun."
—Jason Starr, author of *Bust*, *Slide*, and *The Max*

EVERYONE'S PLAYING AN ANGLE IN THE CITY OF ANGELS

Mad World tells the stories of a black hitman who doubles as a university professor, a Catholic priest who longs to be a gangster, a would-be author from Kansas, a gay phone sex operator who claims he's straight, a group of rich twentysomethings playing a deadly game of life and death, a vicious Mafia boss, and a sleazy Hollywood movie director. As each of their stories intersect, the body count piles up and the action comes nonstop in this tense, white-knuckle thriller by first-time author Andy Rausch.

"A wild ride. If you like it gangster, *Mad World* delivers."
—Daniel Birch, author of *Get Some*

Burning Bulb
PUBLISHING

BLOODLETTING: A TALE OF REVENGE BY ANDY RAUSCH

"Relentless… Addictive… The kind of nightmare you don't want
to wake up from."
—Heywood Gould, screenwriter of *Rolling Thunder*

He was just an average Joe. But when he finds his family held at
gunpoint by merciless thugs, he's told he must murder a Mafia
chieftain if he ever wishes to see his loved ones again.

Against all odds, Joe keeps his end of the bargain, but the criminals
don't. Now at his wits end, Joe is pushed beyond his breaking point
and forced to exact bloody revenge against those who've done him
and his family wrong in this powerful and violent novella by author
Andy Rausch (*Mad World*).

"Andy Rausch has a tight noir style that combines gritty, realistic drama
with a cinematic flair that makes for a powerful, compelling (somewhat
Stephen Kingesque), authentically visual reading experience."
—Stephen Spignesi, author of *Dialogues*

Burning Bulb
PUBLISHING

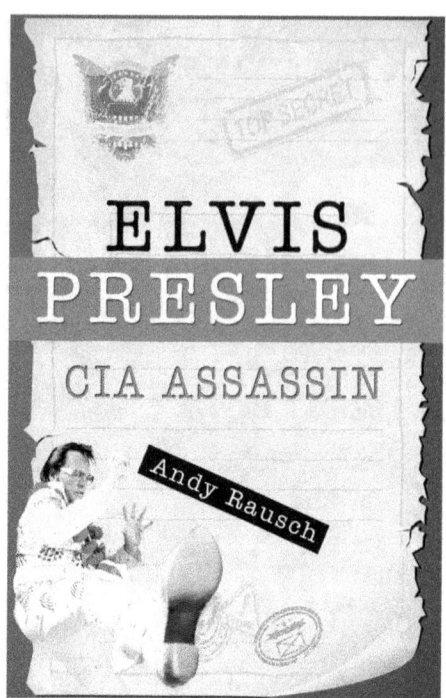

ELVIS PRESLEY, CIA ASSASSIN BY ANDY RAUSCH

"I can guarantee you. Read this book and you'll never look at Elvis the same way again!"
~ Douglas Brode, author of ELVIS CINEMA AND POPULAR CULTURE

SOON TO BE A MAJOR MOTION PICTURE

In 1970, singer Elvis Presley secretly met with President Richard Nixon. This new comedic novel imagines that Presley became a Central Intelligence Agency operative, eventually moving up through the ranks to become a skilled assassin.

Presented in an oral history fashion, the book tells us about Presley's secret transformation by the people who knew him best.

Did he fake his death in 1977? Was Presley involved with the Watergate scandal? The Iran hostage crisis? Communicating with aliens?

Read this book to find out the answers to these and many more questions.

Burning Bulb
PUBLISHING

OTHER GREAT TITLES FROM

Burning Bulb
PUBLISHING

WWW.BURNINGBULBPUBLISHING.COM

ANTHOLOGIES
BIZARRO AND TRANSGRESSIVE FICTION

THE BIG BOOK OF BIZARRO

The Big Book of Bizarro brings together the peculiar prose of an international cast of the most grotesquely-gonzo, genre-grinding modern writers who ever put pen to paper (or mouse to pad), including:

NIGHT OF THE LIVING DEAD horror writers John Russo & George Kosana; HUSTLER MAGAZINE erotica contributors Eva Hore, Andrée Lachapelle, & J. Troy Seate and established Bizarro genre authors D. Harlan Wilson, William Pauley III, Wol-vriey, Laird Long, Richard Godwin and so many more!

From Alien abductions to Zombie sex, The Big Book of Bizarro contains OVER FIFTY STORIES of the most outrélandish transgressive fiction that you'll ever lay your capricious and curious hands upon!

WARNING: This book may be one of the most controversial and dangerous books you'll ever read.

WESTWARD HOES

Nine outlaw writers rode into town from obscurity to pen nine tantalizing tales of horror and fantasy, and leaving once they branded their own personal marks on the weird western genre and became living legends of the American Frontier experience.

Like drunken Indian scouts, the writers fervidly tracked down and captured the Western genre, tore off its fashionable veneer and ravished its exposed essence.

So belly up to the bar with your favorite soiled dove and enjoy perusing these thrilling tales of Old West debauchery, danger and desire; compiled by the publisher of The Big Book of Bizarro and featuring the bizarro novella *Big Trouble in Little Ass* by Wol-vriey.

Burning Bulb
PUBLISHING

ANTHOLOGIES
BIZARRO AND TRANSGRESSIVE FICTION

THE BIG BOOK OF BIZARRO SPECIAL KINDLE EDITIONS

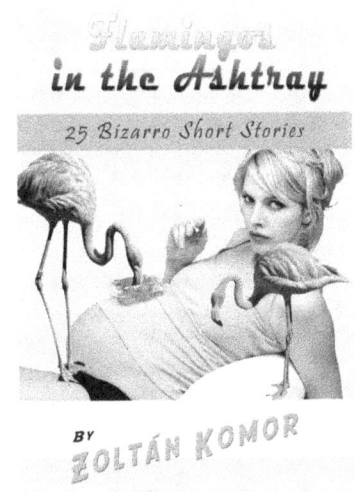

Burning Bulb
PUBLISHING

GARY LEE VINCENT'S
DARKENED
THE WEST VIRGINIA VAMPIRE SERIES

DARKENED HILLS

When evil descends on a small West Virginia town, who will survive?

Jonathan did not start out his life to become a rambler, it just worked out that way. William was a troubled youth with something to hide. Both were from Melas, a small town tucked away in the West Virginia hills... a town where disappearances are happening more and more frequently.

After the suicide of a wanted serial killer, the townsfolk thought the nightmare was over. But when a centuries-old vampire is discovered they find out the hard way it's just getting started. Dark secrets can only stay hidden for so long and when the devil comes to collect, there will be hell to pay. Can Jonathan and William find a way to stop the vampire before it's too late? Find out in *Darkened Hills!*

DARKENED HOLLOWS

In the heart-stopping sequel to the award-winning *Darkened Hills*, Jonathan and William must return to West Virginia to face possible criminal charges stemming from their last visit to the damned town of Melas, where both had narrowly escaped the clutches of a vampire seethe.

And as livestock start mysteriously getting murdered with all of their blood drained, worried farmers are searching for answers - leaving the local Sheriff and his deputy racing against time to learn the cause before a more violent crime is committed.

WWW.DARKENEDHILLS.COM

GARY LEE VINCENT'S
DARKENED
THE WEST VIRGINIA VAMPIRE SERIES

DARKENED WATERS

When the world goes to hell, the chosen must arise!

As Talman Cane orchestrates a flood of epic proportions in this third installment of the *Darkened* series the towns of Melas and Tarklin are caught completely off guard by the deluge. Hell-bent on finishing what they started, the evil brothers return to the lunatic asylum to take care of the witnesses and add to the ever-growing army of the undead.

Aided by Lucifer himself and the insane vampire demon Legion, the stage is set to channel all of the forces of hell to come forth. In an all-out race to survive, Jonathan, William, and Amanda soon discover they are up against impossible odds as Lucifer opens the Gateway to Hell, ushering in the zombie apocalypse and the End Times.

DARKENED SOULS

Melas and the Madison House are about to be rebuilt.
True evil is about to be reborne!

Young ex-priest and vampire-killer William is drawn back to the West Virginian town that almost killed him, where his vampire arch-enemy Victor Rothenstein still stalks the earth.

The town of Melas lies destroyed after the battle of the End of Days. But why is wealthy Jackie Nixon so eager to rebuild it using the bone dust of murdered souls?

Terrible evil has visited before, but the Gateway to Hell is about to be reopened in a horrific climax. And this time – it's personal.

WWW.DARKENEDHILLS.COM

Burning Bulb
PUBLISHING

WEST VIRGINIA-THEMED HUMORROROTICA

BY RICH BOTTLES JR.

HELLHOLE WEST VIRGINIA

From the heights of Mothman's perch high atop the Silver Bridge in Point Pleasant to the depths of Hellhole Cavern in Pendleton County, evil lurks within the shadows as the sun sets upon the haunted hills and hollows of West Virginia.

Bizarro author Rich Bottles Jr. blows the coffin lid off horror genre clichés with this tour de force cast of Eco-friendly vampires, beach-yearning zombies and sex-starved she-devils.

LUMBERJACKED

If you are easily offended or do not possess a truly depraved sense of humor, this story may not be the light summer reading fare you desire. As for the four feisty female freshmen stranded on top of West Virginia's third highest mountain, they have no choice but to experience the sick, twisted debauchery and perverted mayhem described deep inside the tight unbroken bindings of this horrific missive.

Lumberjacked takes the reader to a nightmarish world where character development and aesthetic integrity are prematurely cut short by the swinging axes of maniacal lumberjacks, who are hell bent on death and destruction in the remote forests of Appalachia. And at the climax, when paranoia crosses over to the paranormal, Lumberjacked makes Deliverance look like a family raft trip down the Lower Gauley.

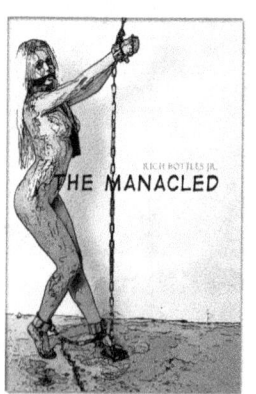

THE MANACLED

What happens when twin brothers lease out the former West Virginia State Penitentiary with the false purpose of filming a documentary on supernatural phenomena, but their true intention is to make a pornographic movie?

Chaos ensues as the disturbed spirits of murdered convicts, along with the reanimated dead from the neighboring Indian Burial Mound, take their vengeance on the unwary and undressed trespassers.

Zombies, ghosts, mobsters and porn collide in this bizarro tale from horror author Rich Bottles Jr.

Burning Bulb
PUBLISHING

WOL-VRIEY
BIZARRO AND TRANSGRESSIVE FICTION

Burning Bulb
PUBLISHING

BOSTON POSH

In 2028 AD, the USA is a nation ravaged by hungry dragons and dinosaurs. In Boston, Massachusetts, private eye Bud Malone is hired to rescue a kidnapped heiress. But nothing is as it seems. Malone works to unravel a tangled web involving Boston China-town, a 200-year-old woman with a 9-year-old body, white robots, a human-liver-eating psychopath, a golem, a porcelain dragon, and a snake goddess with a crush on him. There's also a woman obsessed with chicken sex. Then Malone meets Posh Lane, a gorgeous call girl who's desperate to quit her pimp. Romantic sparks ignite be-tween Posh and Malone, but Posh's past suddenly catches up with her in a BIG way. To save Posh, Malone agrees to run a quest for Earth's new rulers, the Forks. But, Malone has no idea that agree-ing to the Fork's odd request will send him on the weirdest trip he's ever been on in his life.

VEGAN VAMPIRE VAGINAS

The biggest bank heist in US history. And Tom Palmer can't remember pulling it off. And no, this isn't your standard case of amnesia. After a one-night-stand gone horribly wrong, Boston salesman Tom Palmer wakes up with a vagina implanted in his left hand. Then his day gets worse:

Tom is transported across space-time to a nightmare version of Boston, one where the Bizarro virus has transformed half the population into cannibals. Worst of all, Tom discovers that in this new Boston, he's the infamous gangster Pussypalm, wanted for robbing the Federal Reserve Bank of Boston a year ago. He also learns that the vagina in his hand is prophetic, i.e. it talks . . . after sex. With 130 people left dead during his bank heist and six billion dollars missing, Tom knows he's living on borrowed time. It is in his best interests not to remember anything. Because once he does . . .

VEGAN ZOMBIE APOCALYPSE

In the post-apocalypse worlderness, zombies rule the earth. They're allergic to meat, and brains literally make them explode. Zombies now eat blood potatoes, parasitic tubers grown in the flesh of humancows corralled in maximum security farms. Two fugitives meet in the ancient ruins of Texas. The first is Soil 15-f, a womancow who's escaped her farm a week before she's due to be killed and her blood potato crop harvested. The second fugitive is Able Kane, former head necros food technician, now sentenced to death for heresy. But Soil is no ordinary humancow. Unknown to herself, she's the vegan zombie agricultural revolution, and the zombies desperately want her back. And the necros equally desper-ately want Able Kane dead. He's fled with a forbidden discovery which will reshape the world for the worse if used. And Able is just hardheaded/misguided enough to use it.

THE FALL OF TOMORROW

Hopelessness... How do you protect your loved ones when Hell itself opens its insidious mouth?

Horror... Nightmarish Creatures invade your world and there is nowhere to hide.

Blood... How long can you hold out before they come for you?

Pain... Where do you run to avoid being eaten alive by monsters with a voracious appetite for your flesh?

Screams... While you selfishly run for your own life.

Questions... Who is to blame? Where did they come from? How many people survived...and how does the human race find the means to fight back?

THE FALL OF TOMORROW is man's last tale of desperation told by those that are striving to salvage some hope against a ravenous bastion of evil beasts bent on ruling our world.

"David Fairhead writes compelling stories that offer very human characters and very inhuman monsters. There is no subtlety in Fairhead's imagination - he is simply dying to scare the hell out of you."
- Nelson W Pyles - author of DEMONS, DOLLS AND MILKSHAKES

Burning Bulb
PUBLISHING

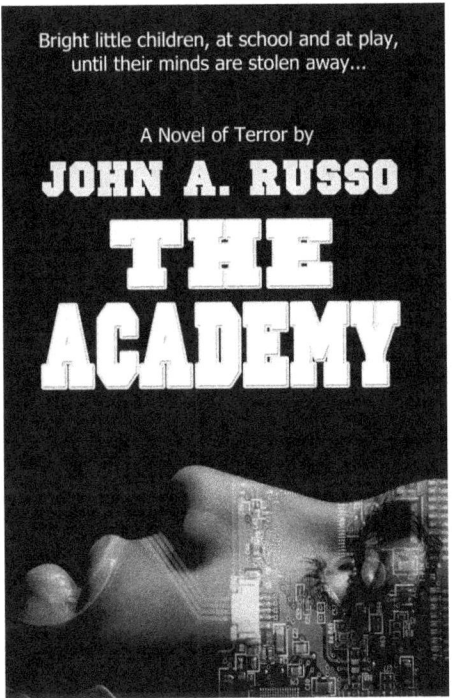

THE ACADEMY

The Academy. It's every parent's dream, turning their little darlings into geniuses, superachievers, perfect little children.

And if there's a problem, the Academy fixes that too. It's a simple operation. Just a little device. Then a teeny pink scar on a tender little skull . . .

One boy knows the secret. Now he wants his mind back. But it's much, much too late. Too late for anything but the ugly feelings. The bad feelings. The messy sexy feelings. The knife-cold hatred, the murderous rage, for total, screaming, blood-drenching revenge . . .

www.TheJohnRusso.com

Burning Bulb
PUBLISHING

DEALEY PLAZA

From legendary horror and suspense writer JOHN RUSSO comes a harrowing tale where no one is safe!

Dealey Plaza is one of the most notorious places in America, and when youthful conspiracy buffs go there in 1964 to stage their own reenactment of the Kennedy Assassination, four of them are brutally murdered -- the first victims of a hate-filled legacy that continues for four more decades.

The survivors of that long-ago Dallas trip, each of them now icons of the American way of life, are about to be honored -- or killed.

Who will live and who will die? Will it be country-western star Lori McCoy? Her loving husband? Her scheming ex-husband? Or the case-hardened FBI agent and longtime friend who risks his life trying to protect them?

www.DealeyPlazaBook.com

Burning Bulb
PUBLISHING

www.ingramcontent.com/pod-product-compliance
Lightning Source LLC
Chambersburg PA
CBHW070803120626
46557CB00002B/693